Another Yellow Door

By

C Faherty Brown

Cover Design By:

C Faherty Brown

Prologue ~

I had lived a 'normal' life. The kind of life where you subscribed to the get up and go to work, pay your bills, buy stuff, do things on the weekend if you weren't too tired. Have relationships. Answer everyone's questions that start with "when are you going to...."

I was slowly fading away in this life.

Then I sold everything that I had purchased to fit into that norm. I lived in a friend's basement. I saved money. I made plans. I packed up and moved to an island off the coast of Ireland. I spent months living on an island that had not been inhabited full time for decades. An island where once, life was lived within a community. A small community. People interacted with and depended on one another, whether they wanted to or not. Rich with story tellers, true characters of life, and beauty that was bordered by treacherous ocean waves and storms.

I couldn't stay forever. So I left. But I still dream about it.

I.

I return.

Every night while I sleep I leave where I am-and go. I go to a place, but even more than that, I go to what I liked about myself. Not trying to sound dramatic or morose. Just truthful. I liked myself best when I was existing in a place I felt connected to. I've discovered that to some, not all, place is a very important part of their existence.

My place, so far, is that island in the Atlantic Ocean. There was a connection. Most who went there to visit stayed a couple of hours. Some, stayed overnight. Some, stayed for extended days. The majority of the world, I assume but I feel I am correct, doesn't even know of its existence. I stayed for months, extending my life there for as long as I could. I wasn't ready to leave.

I only left because I had to.

I returned to this life amidst little, very little, fanfare. Lives didn't stop because of my absence. I didn't expect them to. But there was a realization I hadn't expected-lives *didn't change* because of my absence.

That kinda hurt. A little. Until I changed my perspective about it. On reflection I wasn't surprised. I lived a peripheral existence to most people's lives. I wasn't the center of, or much of a cog in, other's existence. There was relief when I realized this and accepted that it was 'me' not anyone else.

Life was as pleasant as I wanted it to be or as frustrating as I allowed it to become.

It didn't take more than a few days (hours if I am being completely honest) to confirm what I knew when I had left and then when I had returned. I couldn't do 'this'. I could not live like *this*. Life is not supposed to be a trap. But we keep building our own traps. I struggle with this. I did see that the lives many were building were exactly what they wanted and thrived in. I both envied them and knew without any doubt that that was not for me.

I returned to my friend's basement where I had lived prior to finding peace on that Irish island. I lived on very little. I had managed to return with more money than expected. Though I had savings put aside specifically for getting restarted upon my return from Ireland, I had more than I had anticipated. While living there I had felt very little need to buy much other than food and books and pay rent (and I worked some of that off).

Life took on that numbing indifference when I returned. But it was tolerable. I took on two jobs. Other than the minimal rent my friend accepted from me and the cost of my food I spent nothing, and saved more.

Slowly a plan, a 'non-plan', took shape. I knew what kind of life I didn't want but hadn't yet formulated how to create the life I wanted. I knew it wouldn't be living in a basement, or working day in and day out to pay for a life that dulled my every sense. Maybe that isn't accurate. I couldn't find the peace here that I found there. There I was busy, creative and interactive with the world in every sense that I could be. Here there was too much.

Too much stimulation. Too much chaos. It was difficult to be part of the world. Maybe it was quite the opposite of being dulled. Maybe it was just the 'too much' that kept me from being able to be a part of it. A hyper life is too much for me.

One late evening after working a full shift at two different jobs I sat watching Youtube to fall asleep. Videos kept being suggested about tiny homes-I had some interest so I watched. Then videos about 'van life' would be suggested. So I watched them. That night, I watched many of them. I became enamored with the idea of it. Enough so that I wanted to make it more than an idea. An idea grew into a possible option. An option grew into a plan. A plan grew into action.

What little time off I had I spent with purpose. Time with people I cared for or time looking for a van. To live in. I found what I wanted after only three weeks of researching. Then I searched until I found a used one. A large cargo van. Clean and empty with low miles. The time I had been using to search for a van now turned into time learning how to do what I wanted to do with the van and searching out what I would want in the van. I became addicted to videos on van life, tiny-home life and self-sustained living. Travel blogs and vlogs were how-to bibles for figuring out how to do this. Eventually the time I spent on research turned into hands on work. All of the work was with one focus in mind. To create my own space to live in and go.

It took 19 months. I learned how to, or helped someone helping me, run electric/solar power, plumbing, put in insulation, line walls with wood slats, install lights, everything I needed. It felt empowering to have a hand (or paid a hand) in creating everything. From nothing.

The van held everything I needed. There was a bathroom, kitchen, bedroom, living room and garage. I even had an 'outside shower'. Not to mention storage. It would probably be okay to put the word 'miniscule' in front of every 'room'. I worked on the floor plan for a long time to have everything I needed and wanted, without compromising. This was a home. The first thing I knew I wanted, but was one of the last things completed, was my entrance. Technically there were four entrances. But the main entrance of the 'home' was through the sliding side door. When the van was completed the side door of the van slid open bringing into view the front 'wall' of my home. A window that slid up and down, opening like any house window. To the right of the window was a door. An actual door like any house. The door was a dutch door. I could open the top and leave the bottom closed. Or vice versa. Or open them together.

I painted the door yellow.

When the double back doors of the van were open you were in the 'garage'. Under part of the bed was a storage high enough and large enough to put my bicycle with the front tire removed. There was a small cook stove, extra water storage, a solar generator, and a wooden bench. When I was parked I could pull the bench out and put it to the right of my 'front door'.

The inside of the van was simple and clean and all wood of some kind. The bed was smaller than most beds I saw in vans converted for living because I only needed a fixed single bed for me. This left more room for other areas in the van. It felt spacious and gave me room to actually move. I had a separate sitting 'area' with a chair so I didn't have to always sit on the bed. I had a chest refrigerator that could also be used as a cooler in the event I was off grid for long periods and didn't want to use up power. There was a table that pivoted/folded/maneuvered to my sitting area and could be removed for other areas, to add space to the kitchen prep area or to give me a place to write or eat while sitting on the bed. The kitchen was outfitted with everything I needed to cook, to eat, to prep. A small toaster oven was packed in one of the drawers. Likely it would only be used if I was tied into the grid. I had 2 induction burners. All of the bits and pieces you need to feed yourself.

As the van became more and more equipped I spent more time in it. I learned so much by being part of the build. It was comforting to know if something went wrong chances were good if I couldn't fix it I would at least have an understanding of what needed done. It felt like practice when I would cook in the van or use the composting toilet. The bathroom was a complete bathroom. I couldn't hook the toilet up to running water even if I had the accommodations to do so, but the sink and shower I could. Otherwise I had a 40 gallon tank for clean water. I was prepared to be fully off grid. It was also a good way to see if what I was doing was going to be functional. Some changes were made to the original ideas along the way of the build.

When I was ready to go, finally, I sold my car. That put more money in the bank to my saved funds, to live on. Family and friends had a large cookout to say good bye again. There were a few who thought I was "ridiculous" for thinking I could live like this. Why don't I settle down some asked covertly, some asked out right.

There were those who didn't understand but were curious and even excited.

There were those who wanted to do something like what I was doing but hadn't made the decision to change their lives.

It's kind of funny. Not 'ha-ha' funny but chuckle because I don't know how else to acknowledge it funny. But funny that I can't figure out my place in life. I can't find that comfort. Truth be told I did find it I just couldn't keep it. So I'm trying to replicate it in another time and another way.

I had strictly forbidden anyone giving me gifts. But they had all pitched in and had gotten me some gas cards and groceries and an envelope with some cash. If nothing else I could consider it emergency funds they said.

Nice. Food and gas. I would use it.

I left.

Because I needed to.

Again.

II.

I drove back roads. Though I had been driving the van to practice driving around in something this size, it still took some getting used to. My little 2 door car had given way to a vehicle 3 times its size.

There is something liberating about driving with the window down and your arm hanging out. My first day I drove over 200 miles to a campground I had chosen as my destination. It wasn't fancy, it was small but very clean. I passed a few camping sites that were set up with tents or campers as I headed to my site but didn't see another soul. I paid my one night fee by shoving cash in a locked box on the post at the end of the site I chose. No one was set up close to anyone else so I picked an isolated spot as well. It was wrapped in evergreens but for the 'frontage' of the site that was open to the gravel parking area.

My first cooked on the road dinner was oatmeal with chia seeds, dried cranberries and honey. I built a small fire in the stone fire pit, set the bench by yellow door and did some stretches to work out the kinks from sitting for so long.

My intention was to write my on-going, on-line, journal that I started when I was in Ireland. I had tracked my progress with the van and retained some of my readers from when I wrote from an island. Island living seemed to be of more interest than working on a van. People didn't read or engage like they did when I wrote from the island. Today was day 1 and regardless if I had one reader (me) or one thousand I wanted to track this and my thoughts. I propped my computer on the hood of the van to type. I did not want to sit down again. I included a picture of my first night set up complete with the bench by yellow door. Some of my friends out there in internet world would appreciate the connection. When I was finished I walked around the little campsite and picked up sticks and nature's debris and added it to the fire. I set up my little camping stove and made some lemon-ginger tea. As homage to an island-very far away, and to a people-of very long ago, I made it a whiskey tea. I toasted my inauguration. My first night. And the spirit of those who may be watching over me.

It felt wonderful. The small amount of whiskey added a small amount of heat as it traveled down my throat. The aroma of the fire, the trees, even the mold of the damp area all added to an enriched feeling of being surrounded, almost closed in. Not like being closed in a room. But being enveloped in a cocoon of comfort.

Eventually I sat on the bench. Staring at the fire I couldn't help but imagine the ocean below me instead of pine trees around and above me.

Soon though, mingled with the crackle of the fire I became aware of the voices around me. Crickets. Frogs. Occasionally a sound that I would later learn to differentiate from other animals-coyotes. When I first parked I found the spot to be quiet. By the time I kicked dirt over the embers of the fire I was acquainting myself with these night noises.

In the van I washed off the smoke smell and made my home comfortable and tidy. I liked it like that. The kettle was ready to be turned on in the morning and white tea was ready to be brewed. My dishes from dinner were washed and put away. I crawled into my bed with the cozy duvet, the vent above me open for fresh air. From the little shelf above the bed I grabbed a book "On An Irish Island" and read by the portable solar powered light. When I woke, my first full day on the road, my nose was stuffy, I was a little sore, but eager. I put on the tea kettle and stepped out into the still smokey-smelling-tree-enclosed campsite. It was barely dawn.

It felt good to not have to be somewhere. Almost two years of working two jobs and working on the van had taken every ounce of energy I had.

I retrieved the small folding table from under the bed storage that I could reach from inside and set it up in front of the bench outside. It was chilly so I pulled on my wool 'jumper' aka 'sweater' and sat with my cup of tea and my computer. I pulled up a map and got a look at where I wanted to head out and explore. No destination…yet. Just go.

I checked emails. My friends Leo and Pilar were still hoping to persuade me to visit them. Leo had been a business man for over 20 years. He sold most of what he had built up and they had bought a ranch.   Maybe I would head in their general direction. Maybe not.   Many of the emails I had were from friends I had met on a 1.66 square mile piece of rock in the Atlantic Ocean.   People from around the world.   Ealga and Gregory were now in Scotland for a residency for Gregory's art and sending me their best on my new journey.   Niall was still working with his father Cashel who wouldn't do much in the way of emails but sent his best wishes via Niall.   Hannah sent me pictures of the two of us and wished me safe travels.   They all said in their different ways they hoped I would return.   They hoped these travels made a path back to where they felt I belonged.   I agreed with everything I had, I had found a 'place' where I fit.   I lay my hand on the messages-wanting to feel the words that originated thousands of miles away but found me no matter where I went.   I responded to everyone.

Then I packed up.   Left.

I randomly chose Utah as a direction to head in from the places I had hoped to go see.   I plugged in one of the state parks as a destination on my GPS.   I had it set so there would be no freeways.   I kept notebooks on the passenger seat. I wrote names of towns, or names of people on the signs outside of towns. Signs that said 'welcome to (any town) home of (hometown boy or hometown girl). Evenings I would look up the towns or the hometown peoples. It was a fascinating way to learn some local histories. Some more interesting than others.

I stopped for gas and breakfast after driving long enough to get sore again. I stopped at a gas station that reminded me of a cottage. It had flowers hanging outside. And flower boxes around the permitter of the building. There were picnic tables with umbrellas in the yard adjacent to the building. There were a couple of houses nearby, just down the road.

I hoped to grab something simple inside, even a donut, but was pleasantly surprised to find the owner behind the counter and fresh made egg/cheese/bacon/biscuits being cooked on a griddle. I ordered three sandwiches to go. They smelled good enough to eat now and later in the day for lunch or dinner. While the man behind the counter was making my sandwiches he casually asked me how my day was looking and what it was going to be like. A more curious question than 'how are you'. I told him it was my first full day of a new journey.

He looked up from the sandwich making and wrapping. He struck me as very handsome. He smiled and said "tell me more, I'm Mason". I replied "I'm Bronagh". While he finished up and rang up my purchase he listened to my story. He followed me out to the van and I showed him my world on wheels. He asked if he could show his wife and son. I had no desire to refuse, he pulled out his cell phone and called his wife asking her to come to the station. Mason nodded his head and I looked in the direction he nodded to a small white house closest to the store/gas station. A beautiful little place with flowers, trees and toys. A swing to relax in, and a swing set big enough for adults.

Soon enough I was meeting Emmy his wife and "Jar" his son. It took me a minute to figure out "Jar" was a nickname to go with his father's name. Mason. Jar.

Emmy was too polite to invade my space but Jar accepted my invitation to go in with his parent's permission. I had Jar open doors and drawers showing his parents, who remained outside but peering in, the ingenuity of my home. Jar was bored soon enough and went back to his yard to play. Mason and Emmy invited me to sit with them at one of the tables and tell them about my journey. I accepted and brought my sandwiches to the table. Mason disappeared into the store and returned with three cups of coffee.

While I ate they told me their story. They met right after high school. Mason went to school for IT. He was great with computers and quickly absorbed all that came along. He loved the new technologies and how fast they developed. He worked his way through college. Though he loved the technology part, and the work part, he did not enjoy the stress part. He and Emmy married. Financially they were sound. Doing very well. Emmy worked in a daycare and loved being around the children. Emmy saw Mason changing. He became quiet, withdrawn. I looked at Mason sitting across from me, next to Emmy. The two of them seemed so at ease with one another, comfortable. His eyes were bright, his smile-easy. He came home one night and Emmy asked him if he was happy. He said no without even having to think about it. They came here. They bought the station from Emmy's uncle and made a good life. A happy life. It had different stresses but shared stresses. Jar ran over and sipped from Emmy's coffee. He ran back to the play set and hung upside down.

I shared my story. I gave them a yellow card, with my contact information and how they can follow my journey if they wished. When we parted for the day I knew I had new friends. Pictures were taken, hands were shook. Smiles were shared. At no time did Mason or Emmy express jealousy or envy. They loved what I was doing. But they loved it as my story. They had found their journey. That helped me put in perspective, maybe even better define, me and what I am doing. My story. I'm finding it, writing it, living it. Others are doing the same.

As I pulled away I felt something I hadn't felt in some time. Purpose. Excitement. Simply-joy. I looked on the GPS for how many miles to Utah.

This was going to be a very long drive. I turned on some music and smiled.

At my second stop of the day I ate my second sandwich from Mason and I started my first notebook. I scrawled across the top "The Peoples" with an after thought I wrote "From The Road". Up in the corner I wrote "#1". I knew there would be more than one notebook full of people. I had parked at a town park and was sitting at another picnic table. I wrote about Mason, Emmy and Jar. I sat at the table and let thoughts find their way in. I looked around the quiet park. Unfamiliar though similar to so many other places.

I was often asked as it became more apparent to people I would actually be leaving again, if I wasn't scared to be on my own. As my eyes roamed the park I tried to form an honest answer. I grabbed a different notebook to jot my thoughts down.

Am I scared? No. I don't exist in a permanent state of fear. I do 'get' scared. I looked up, looked around. There was nothing to suggest I should be scared. I tried to think of the last time I was scared.

I put the pen down and dropped my chin into my hand propped up on the table.   I thought my thoughts. Fear.

I had found a place where I knew how to exist.   I could talk to people, I could be alone, I could be in groups, I could test myself and push at my limits- both physical and mental.   I felt like 'me' there. Then, I had to leave.

And I was scared.

Scared about returning to a life that made me nervous, uncomfortable and often times-dull.   I was scared I couldn't do it.   I didn't want work to be life. I didn't mind working to pay for life.   But I didn't want work to take over and *be* life.   I was scared of this.   I made a compromise.   I worked a lot for almost two years to be able to do 'this'.   I was careful with my money.   I did what I could do in building the van, others helped, there was little I had to pay others to do.   I don't mind 'work' I just struggle finding my purpose in the work I do (did).   I enjoy doing a good job whatever my work was, there is reward in that and I took pride in that. But...

I tried to remember other times I was scared. Most of what I could recall was probably more along the lines of being uncomfortable. I may have parlayed discomfort into fear. This would take more thought. I either lived with less fear than I thought or I wasn't being honest with myself.

I cleaned up my minimal meal mess and picked up some trash that had fallen out of or never made it into the park's trash receptacle. My little way of thanking the town for use of its park. It never hurts to leave a place a little better then how you found it. I had my sites set on a small waterfall about two hours away. The day turned more grey as I drove. No rain fell but it sure looked threatening. Even with my practice driving I had not driven the van in much more than a sprinkle.

After an hour of driving I passed a homemade sign that said HONEY AHEAD. I slowed as I approached a sign that said HONEY HERE. There was a stand set up in a yard next to a driveway. I backed the van in, another benefit to appreciate less traveled back roads.

On the stand was a metal box with a hole cut in the top with a $ sign pasted above it. There was a squeeze bottle of honey and a box of crackers. A little note taped to the table said "try it first!" So I did. After a taste of the best honey I ever had I picked up two jars of honey from crates under the stand. The sign said $5 a jar. I slid a ten dollar bill into the box. I would love to get all of my foods like this.

When I made it to the empty parking lot for the waterfall I got my hiking stick, sling bag with snacks, water and notebook and my hiking boots. It was a little exciting to have everything I need right here with me. I locked up the van and checked the trail information posted at the trail head. It was about a 2 mile hike to the falls. It was still cloudy and grey but warm. I had a good sweat going when I reached the falls. I was on the lower trail and no one else was there. I counted myself lucky to be here instead of going from one job to another. I felt like I was still decompressing from that.

The water was falling alright. It wasn't huge, maybe 30 to 40 feet high. But it was falling fast and hard, there must have been a good deal of rain recently. I stood on the very edge of dry land, the beach to the body of water at the foot of the falls. The spray felt wonderful but it only hit me sporadically. The rim above was heavy with foliage and trees. The boulders and cave like formations around me called to be played in. I wondered if they were ever used for habitation. I crawled into a few of them, exploring. I sat in one looking out of the almost circular entrance. What a pretty frame to the world. I imagined sleeping here. Listening to the water falling. Hollering out to the neighbors. I wonder if cave dwellers hollered hello to their neighbors. I'll say yes. Because they would have depended on one another and been friendly.

I made my way back to the van. I sat down inside with my computer and tried to look up the rules about camping here. I found the website but it was pretty bland. It didn't state any rules or regulations. There was nothing posted in the parking lot. I moved the van so it was close to the edge of the parking lot and backed it in so I just had to pull out in the morning. I didn't set up camp or unpack anything that I would if I was planning to stay in place. I opened the doors to let the breeze blow through. I had one sandwich left from Mason. I ate it cold with a glass of tea from the full glass jug in the refrigerator. A gallon of sun tea was about the last thing I prepped before leaving yesterday. Was it just yesterday? I ate an apple and a few strawberries.

After cleaning up dinner I sat to write. I wrote as honestly as I could about fear and being scared vs. being uncomfortable. By the time I finished that piece and then wrote about today with Mason, Emmy and Jar I posted my blog and enjoyed reading what some of my friends were up to.

Leo and Pilar sent me a picture of a gravel patch at their ranch. My guest room. Great minds do think alike because Ealga and Gregory sent me a picture from their current location in Scotland, also a gravel patch next to the house they were renting with the caption "waiting on your arrival". I put the coffee pot on to make a late day cup of coffee. Hour of the day be damned. Another pure joy. Drink coffee when I want without worry it's too late. I used the French press and enjoyed a wonderful cup of coffee well after 8 pm. I put the remainder of the coffee in a mason jar to make iced coffee in the morning.

I carried my nighttime routine with me no matter where I went. I locked up the van from the inside. I showered, which is different in a van than in a house but still a luxury. Water didn't remain running. I got wet, soaped up, then rinsed off in my wet room/ bathroom. Everything in the bathroom would be soaked if it wasn't water proofed behind what I thought were genius designs. With everything and myself tidied up I lay down to watch music on Youtube as I fell asleep.

The caffeine and/or fear kicked in at 2:57 am. Without being sure why my eyes flew open at 2:57 am while the Weepies were singing "Can't Go Back Now". Something told me to get up and go. I got up and started to make sure everything was shut and locked down but something kept saying "GO" in my head. I briefly thought about getting dressed but the urgency in my head stressed the "GO" again. I crawled into the driver's seat and went.

As I drove out of the parking lot I felt hyper alert to take notice of anything I could see that may have set off my internal alarms. It was too dark to see anything outside of the scope of the the headlights. I hadn't noticed any other vehicles when I was leaving. I half expected something to jump in front of the van.

Nothing did.

My heart was racing. It took an hour of driving and listening to the radio to start to feel normal. I drove until I got to a Walmart and parked under a light. I got out and walked around the van just to see if a zombie arm or other monster arm was hanging by a chain or something. I've never watched a zombie movie or read a zombie book, but I understood the concept. Old campfire stories were more likely the source of imagining arms hanging from my van by chains.

There wasn't.

Inside again I locked up, including the sliding door and yellow door and let myself wind down.

Interesting that earlier in the day I couldn't remember anything specific about being scared and then *this* happened. The universe provides doesn't it? Damn coffee.

It was after 9 am when I woke up in the chair with my feet propped up on the bed. I had a headache, stuffy throat and felt all kinds of moods pushing my eyebrows down into furrows. Not wanting to admit it but I was pretty sure the coffee was part of my problem. Also not wanting to admit an old diagnosis of allergies to trees and molds may have been accurate. Though I long scoffed at that diagnosis.

I made my iced coffee from the leftover brew last night and sat down to search out my destination for the day. Maybe a real campsite would be a good idea. And some allergy medicine. I had no desire to face Walmart shopping so I took some ibuprofen hoping it would help. I found a campsite less than 300 miles away. By the time I drove away my head felt lighter and my eyebrows didn't feel like they weighed 2800 pounds.

I couldn't help but rethink my 'fear' thoughts from yesterday. I don't dwell in fear, my mind wasn't changed about that. Though I blame the coffee, and it's possible that focusing my thoughts on fear yesterday was the reason for my reaction at 2:57 am. Maybe there was something else going on last night. I don't disregard or dismiss that we are meant to have instincts and awareness. I didn't dismiss that my instincts said 'get out' for a reason. I may very well have been reacting to something I heard while I was asleep but was not conscious enough to process it.After an hour of driving I pulled into a small town. I wanted to jot down some thoughts. I did that and felt a need to walk. I needed to move.

I drove the van into what appeared to be an old downtown. Many small, and larger, towns are losing their original downtowns (town centers) to areas that are spread out and larger allowing for more traffic and newer buildings. Leaving the downtowns to decline and decay. Town and county services move to more accessible areas. Leaving behind beautiful old buildings for newer, less substantial, buildings.

Fortunately many old downtowns are now seeing revitalization movements. People saw value in the old buildings and the streets designed for people to walk from business to business. Coffee shops, art galleries, restaurants, book stores and community programs were finding their niche in the old store fronts. People were making apartments and condominiums out of the upstairs units. Many of them high end living.

I locked the van and walked the street. Appropriately and not surprising named 'Main Street'. There were a few store fronts covered from within by brown paper. This is usually a sign of something being done inside with the space. There were many second story balconies. There were flowers, some wrought iron chairs and tables, both on the balconies and on the sidewalk in front of businesses. I easily passed by the ice cream shop but couldn't pass by the bakery. I walked in to the comforting smells and walked out eating a blueberry scone-with real and large blueberries surprising and pleasing my tastebuds.

I stopped in front of the bookstore looking at the display of 'new arrivals' until I finished eating my scone. I tossed my napkin in the receptacle and walked to the end of the street. I saw a sign pointing to the 'historical' part of town. I walked a couple of blocks over and found myself standing on a street of homes built long ago. In front of me stood an enormous house built of stone. The sign out front said "Canal County Historical Society". From hooks under that large sign hung a little wooden sign that said "OPEN".

I walked in and put my $2 in the metal box stating there was a $2 admission. The house smelled old. I liked the smell.

I waited to see if someone was going to greet me. Pamphlets about the house and town stood on a counter with a sign saying 'self guided tour'. I took the pamphlets and started walking around. The original owner and builder of the house was born in 1797. He made money in "textiles". He built the home starting in the 1840's. It wasn't finished until the early 1850's. His portrait and portraits of his family hung in what had been the "great room".

That era was not kind to people and their looks. He was surely more attractive than the artist portrayed him. I stared at him. That man who would have stood right here where I stand. With his whole world around him. What did his world look like? There were photographs of him, older, throughout the house. The photographs were a little kinder.

I read more from the pamphlet. He was an abolitionist who supported and created opportunities for many regardless of color or status. He created jobs and he paid for higher education for many. He built a school that was open to anyone and everyone. In a time when not everyone would have supported that.

I looked back to the portrait. Seeing something more than the bushy eyebrows and muttonchops. I felt a little shame for judging his appearance.

Maybe I'm the rare person who finds it fascinating to be in a home the way it would have been nearly 200 years ago. But fascinated I was. No one else was in the house apparently so I felt like it was mine. If only for these few minutes. It was well preserved.

I'm sure the money he spent on furnishings was extravagant and it was made to last. The furnishings were the same in all the pictures. Today you buy a couch and if you don't like it you buy another one in a year or two. Where people used to build and make things to last forever now they are built to *need* replaced within a few years.

If things last people don't make money on selling over and over again.

I made my way to the grand staircase and followed the sign pointing up to the second floor and third floor but said not to go the attic as it is not open to the public. As I neared the top of the staircase to the second floor I heard someone yelling 'hello' from somewhere below. I yelled back "I'm at the top of the stairs" and started to head back down. A woman appeared at the foot of the stairs-breathing a little hard but smiling.

"I'm sorry". Maybe I wasn't supposed to be here. "No no" she waved me to go back. "I'm sorry I wasn't here when you came in. My husband locked himself out of the house without car keys so I ran home to let him in". She waved me to go again. "Go on, I'm down here if you have questions." She smiled and walked away.

I made my way through bedrooms and a study. Bathrooms with original and working plumbing. The first in the state by what the signs said. And signs also asking that visitors not try and prove that the plumbing still works, take their word for it, it does. There are bathrooms downstairs for visitors.

The third floor was for servants of the home. Though the term 'servant' was used due to the time period the folks in this house were more like 'staff'. There were rooms for single people and a couple of rooms for married couples. The rooms had pictures displayed showing the furnished rooms in the late 1800's. They appeared to be very comfortable. Some of the rooms had pictures of the staff who stayed for many years with the family. Many pictures showed the staff and family relaxing together in various parts of the house, including the servants quarters, and the beautiful gardens.

When I made my way back downstairs the same lady was sitting at a desk talking on a cell phone. She told the other person to "hold on a sec" and turned her attention to me. "Do you have any questions hun?"

I said no, but would have continued talking with her if not for her follow up to my answer "thank you for visiting today, I hope you enjoyed it."

I could hear a voice coming from the phone and the lady tried talking to the caller to stop them from talking. She shrugged, rolled her eyes and mouthed "I'm sorry" to me. I smiled and waved goodbye. I made my way back to the van and left the town behind.

Later in the day I found myself parked at another Walmart. I parked in the Timbuktu region of the parking lot. I opened the doors and cooked a meal. In a large pot I dropped a chunk of coconut oil in to melt, chopped mushrooms, onions, red pepper and sautéed it all. I added chicken broth, cooked the pasta, added the pasta. I let it all cook down with seasoning and time. I have to admit, it was good.

Not having much desire to cook most of my life I suddenly found it fascinating. With simple ingredients I chopped and threw together some pretty good meals the past few years. It was while I was trying to save money by not going out to eat that I discovered it was less time consuming to make something then to go out and get something. And there was always plenty for a second meal, or three, out of what I cooked.

I was feeling a little proud of myself.

I lounged back in my sitting area. I was still amazed at the room I had in the van. I had different 'areas' for living, sleeping, cooking, bathroom-ing. It didn't feel small when I wanted to sleep-it felt cozy. When I opened the doors it felt like the outdoors were part of my home. I was a little apprehensive when I started this project. But that seemed now to have been a waste of energy. The things I worried about, which were few were not things that came to fruition. Yet. But I wasn't ruling them out. Mostly it centered around would I get sick of my own and only company. And would I go nuts in this small of a space.

Both issues had easy enough resolutions. One, go find other people to be around. And two, go outside.

I was tempted to close up and go to sleep but it was only an hour to the camp ground. The rest of the drive I was doing a lot of self talk on how great I was going to sleep tonight. I found a drugstore and bought some off-brand allergy medications and some candy.

After registering and getting a map of the local area and the campground I pulled forward to find my spot. This place was beautiful. Immaculately maintained. I followed directions given to me and it felt like I drove for miles. The feeling I got from driving past smiling and waving people was welcome after last night's experience. The sun was finally free of the clouds. The lake was so large I couldn't see the opposite bank.

Though I had intended to spend only one night I think I may stay longer. I found my spot in a campers cul-de-sac. Of the five spots in this area I was only the second occupant. I backed the van in.

I had electric and water hookups so I took advantage of that. The composting toilet was the only thing I couldn't change over to the grid but my shower would benefit from having a new water source. I rolled back the side door to expose yellow door. I set up my bench. I put a table cloth on the-already-there picnic table. I opened the roof vents and turned on the fans. I set up the camp stove on one end of the picnic table and dragged it under the awning that I pulled out over the side entrance. Last I lay the little bamboo outdoor rug in front of the bench.

I set the computer on the hood of the van and wrote about my night fright. Late day caffeine may have been part of the problem but I was pretty sure my instincts were also in play and kicked in for some reason last night.

I painted the picture of events and decided to let the reader decide what transpired. I purposely left the scenario as I drove away from the parking lot at 3 am. I didn't explain anything after that. I posted my words for the world to read. Or not. I retrieved my bicycle and helmet from the garage and decided to pedal around the park.

Campers, the people not the vehicle, seemed to corner part of the market on pleasantness. Everyone I passed spoke to me or waved. The road was so clean and smooth. I pedaled to the lake and walked on the beach. The water was coming in as little rolling waves. I could almost, not quite really, convince myself it was the ocean. It may have worked if I hadn't become intimately close with the ocean. But I have a great imagination and allowed myself the attempt.

I stood still. Closed my eyes. And returned to the ocean. The smells. The wind. The sounds. The seals.

Back at the van a small SUV was parked two spots over and a large tent was already up. I heard laughing from inside.

With windows and yellow door open I sat down with a book. I read a couple of pages and put the book down. After not stopping but to sleep for 19 or more months it was still difficult to sit still. All that time there had been a mental checklist of things to do. Problem was, I'd checked them all off so I could be doing this. I need to fill that void of not having a list.

I had maps in the storage under the passenger seat. One of them was a full map of America. I laid it on the picnic table and weighted it down with rocks. I set up the computer and looked at the big picture. To be honest, I hadn't done this yet.

My plan all along was to not have a plan. But what *am* I going to do?

On the paper map I circled where I started from. I drew a line following the basic routes I had taken thus far. I circled places where I stopped. I was not surprised it wasn't a straight line. I was humored by the shape and different directions.

Currently I have my 'The Peoples' notebook. I have a notebook for thoughts and writing ideas. I took a third notebook and started from day one the places and people, just in list form. Listing where I started and ended up each day. I dated a page for each day so far. Because each day had something to take note of. I suspect there will be days I don't have much to write. But I made a mental note to find something worthy of each day to take note of.

I looked at the paper map. That was a lot of land. I started searching for 'top 10 things to see' in each state. I started a list. I searched for 'most obscure things' to see in each state. I searched for 'things and places to avoid' in each state. Everything I could think of to search and be aware of for each state. I didn't get to each state but I had a folder created on my computer with a subfolder dedicated to each state. Things to see, avoid, hope to see, etc. I added Canada to the list as well. I might not be able to drive to Hawaii but it's on the list.

The map will be marked with where I have actually been. It just won't give me an indication of where I'm going.

Though there were things about some cities that intrigued me I had no desire to drive within large cities. I took a pencil and circled some places on the map that were definitely on the plan. Maybe. Leo and Pilars maybe, the Grand Canyon maybe, Painted Desert maybe, every mountain range maybe, Arches National Park, Crater Lake, Glacier National Park, Montana. Maybe. In my head the places I circled were all ahead of me. On the map they went in every direction, including back in the direction I had come from. I still considered them all ahead of me.

I looked from my map, to my newly formed computer folders, to my notebooks. I have money to do some of this. But surely not nearly all of this. I can always park the van and work, saving money, when I need to. Though it would be a better ~~plan~~ idea to work while I travel and earn money no matter where I go.

I tossed my pen on the table and sat back. Looking at everything made me feel a few things. One, there's a lot I can do and not get bored. Two, there's a lot I could do and never do it all. Three, for not having a plan I seem to have fallen into the trap of trying to create a plan.

What work can I do? I have the computer skills but not sure how to put them to use. I can put this thinking off for today and for tonight but I need a plan. My 'no plan' is temporary and on the way to its demise. Damnit.

I looked up and was surprised I could see lights in the laughing tent and stars up above. I looked at my phone. I'd been sitting her for over three hours. I could hear laughing and music from the tent but had been so focused on what I was doing I hadn't been hearing it. I stepped inside the van and fried an egg and Swiss cheese sandwich. I heard the SUV leave while I was inside. After I ate I rode my bike to the office and bought some firewood. As I pedaled back I made a mental note to find cheaper firewood and store some in the 'garage' of the van. What I bought was strapped to the rack on the back, with room to spare.

I had a small fire going by the time it was fully dark. I used a flashlight to walk the edge of the site and gather up twigs and small branches to make my firewood last a little longer.

I sat by the fire in my camp chair. It was easier to lounge in then on the bench. With my knees nearly even with my chest, my hands dropped in my lap, I quickly fell into the fire's trance.

If you've ever sat at a fire-you know.

I only moved when I had to and that was to feed the fire. This fire sitting was the closest I ever came to being without thought. The more I stared-latching my eyes on to the flame-the less I thought. I think.

I had tried meditation in the past. Everything I did to 'find' mindfulness or focusing on breath, everything I tried, was forced. And I felt nothing but stress trying to achieve this goal of non-thinking.

But light a fire, sit back in a slouchy way and watch the dance of flames. Achieved.

I fed the last piece of wood and watched until the flames gave way to red embers. The embers gave way to ash. The ash gave way to breeze and darkness. I looked around at the night. The moon was doing a bang up job as a night light.

I took the allergy medicine before going to bed hoping to avoid the stuffed-up head in the morning. Not long after I lay down to sleep I heard the neighbors return. The sounds indicated they were happy and having a good time but not being raucous. I was back up and making a cup of tea before 7 am. I made my way back to my lounge chair. A simple tip I had learned was to turn my chair upside down and stick it under the picnic table to avoid getting a wet dew-butt in the morning. It worked. I sat with my tea and the not burning fire-pit.

"Hi". I snapped out of my thoughts and my head up to see a young blonde girl-woman-standing to my left.

"Hi". I was too startled to say much else.

"Sorry, I didn't mean to scare you". She smiled a very dimple inducing smile in apple round cheeks. It invited a smile in return. "I'm Audrey" and she stuck her hand out with grace and confidence. "I" m Bronagh" and stood to take her hand. I stepped to the back of the garage and brought out my spare lounge chair and handed it to Audrey who set it up, also facing the non-burning fire pit. I offered her a cup of tea and she said yes with an eagerness I didn't expect for a cup of tea. I went inside through yellow door and she followed to the door. I offered to let her in and see the van and she said no, she could see most of it.

We sat back down with a cup of tea each. I nodded to the tent and SUV "are you from over there?"

"Yeah. My friends and I are trying to spend a lot of time together. We know we're soon off in different directions."

"Yeah? Where are you going?" I assumed it had to do with graduations and life journeys.

"I graduate in about a month with my BSN".

"So you'll be a nurse?"

"Technically I am a nurse, an LPN. But I will be an RN after graduation and taking the licensure exams."

"Congratulations. That's a lot of work to get here."

She smiled easily. Such confidence in her. "Thanks. But I don't want to be a nurse." She said it so casually and without sadness that it confused me.

"Oh. So why…"

Audrey propped her feet up on the fire pit. Her 'at ease' feeling was enjoyable to watch. I had a feeling she was a pleasure to be around on a regular basis. And before I knew it we were talking like old friends. "My parents wanted me to get a degree. So I did it for them." She shrugged. She turned her head to look at me more than the fire pit. "They feel more secure if I did this before I do what I want."

"What do you want?"

"Well Bronagh" I couldn't help but chuckle at her confidence and comfort in talking with me. I was impressed with her use of my name. "I want to write songs and build stuff."

My reaction made her chuckle in return. "You want to be a carpenter? Or a contractor? Or an engineer?"

"I would love to be a carpenter if I could make a living out of it. All my experience so far is working as a volunteer for Habitat for Humanity. I've learned a lot from the carpenters and builders there. Even some plumbing and electric. But I like working with wood, building things up."

"But you haven't made money?"

"No. And if I never do that's okay. I'll help by volunteering." We talked about this some more and I suggested she look into trade schools. From what I had seen, skilled labor is in high demand. She said she hadn't really thought about that because she was so focused on finishing her BSN but she thought it was a good idea.
"So you will be a full fledge nurse but not a nurse?"

"Well, I'm all in. I told my parents I would do it. They made it easy for me in so many ways. But, they also agreed. If I get a degree they'll help me however they can. I think just knowing they'll support me is enough. And by support I mean encouragement. But, I still have the tests to get through."

"Good luck".

"I know this comes off sounding brash, but I don't need the luck. I put the work in." I raised my tea cup and she saluted back with hers.

"So what about song writing, where does that come in?"

"I write the words, the lyrics. My friends write the music. We've been doing it since grade school."

"How's that going?"

She smiled with those dimply cheeks "pretty good. Haven't sold any but we have a tremendous library. We will. Sell some." And she raised her tea cup first this time with my salute in return.

She asked about the van and what I was doing. I told her. She enjoyed the process I went through to get to the point of the van build, and the van build itself. She asked questions that made me know her interest in building was genuine.

We talked easily while the rest of the world slept. She said her friends would sleep until noon. We talked until I realized how hungry I was. When I offered to make us some breakfast she declined and said she was heading out for a walk. And up she stood and left with a smile. She left me with a chuckle in my spirit. I sat with a cup of coffee and my breakfast at my table inside and responded to emails and comments on my blog.

There was another email from Leo. Aside from the pleasantries he again asked if I would be heading in their direction. He and Pilar were really hoping to see me. I emailed and told him they were one of my few confirmed-possibilities-but-I-have-no-plans-destinations. I had no guarantee yet on when I would be heading in his direction. Or, if.

I headed to the lake on my bike, sling bag on my shoulder with water, snack and notebook. I rode along the lake for an hour or more when I came upon a small shack with a fenced in yard full of kayaks and canoes to rent. It didn't take long for me to get the kayak and life jacket rented and find myself paddling into the lake. From my life jacket's water proof pocket I turned the music on my phone to a Queen playlist. I had a pretty good paddle going to three or four of their songs when "Love of My Life" came on.

I pulled the paddle out of the water and lay it across the kayak in front of me. Me and the kayak just bobbing in the water. I let Freddie sing me into stillness. I lost the energy needed to propel myself forward. I sat rocking gently. Losing my present to my past.

There were boats and other kayaks. None were very close. I turned the music off and paddled back. I turned the kayak in well before the 2 hours I rented it were up, jumped on the bike and went home.

The next two mornings passed. Both mornings Audrey was outside when I woke. I walked out with two mugs of tea and we would sit and talk. She would refuse breakfast and eventually get up and leave to walk.

Both days I went back to the lake and kayaked. I enjoyed the water and the physical exertion. The second day I returned and Audrey's campsite was packed up and gone. She left me a note on yellow door that said "Bronagh, thanks for the morning tea and conversation. I'll be following your journey. Always check who wrote the lyrics. You'll see me in the songs". She drew a smiley face next to her name.

III.

I pulled out the computer to check for my next destination. I felt a need for mountains. I checked for a route and campsites and was heading out in an hour. Two days later I was parked with stocked groceries, firewood and views that would never bore me. The campsite was high in the mountains. The Blue Ridge Mountains were the closest to where I had been. They welcomed me with fantastic weather.

My first night in the mountains I walked with packed sling bag, a camp chair shoved in, and took one of the many trails to promised vistas. It was late so I had a hiking headlamp on in case I didn't get back before dark. If I found a good vista I would not be back before dark.

The trail itself was easy and marked well. It was other-worldly. The trees and foliage made it darker then it really was. The greens and shadows playing and merging together to create a fairy like world.

Until.

I stepped from behind the tree line and found myself on the edge. In front of me, below me, beyond how far I could see-were mountains, covered in the colors of different trees, shaded by clouds above in patches, or in full sunlight where clouds did not exist.

I stood. In awe.

I stood for I don't know how long. I hadn't seen another soul on the trail. I set my chair up and my camera on a mini tripod far enough back from the edge that I felt relaxed and grateful. The night, I knew, was bringing a show.

I had everything in hand's reach. The sling bag and water were leaning up against me. Camera on the other side of me to capture a time lapse. Phone camera and notebook in my lap. I watched the western sky. The beauty of the day could be seen in all its variety. Though there were no rain clouds there were many parts of the world before me that were having a grey or cloudy evening. Their neighbors meanwhile were enjoying a fully sunny day.

Soon enough the sun seemed to pick up speed the closer it got to the horizon. I turned the camera on to capture it in a time lapse.

The closer the sun got to that far away line I could never touch-no matter how long I traveled-colors began to change. And appear. Pale blues, whites and grey of the sky stepped back for orange and yellow to step forward and spread out-from the center to the far reaches. Purple reached out low across the mountains. Coral and misty rose stretched out and up-touching the low reaching aqua that just seemed to develop from azure and emerald deciding to marry. From the very center yellow took center stage. Yellow like no other yellow on earth.

Such a show.

I moved to take a picture with my phone. Catching me by surprise, emotions welled up in me. Without a trace of sadness or upset in my heart-tears rolled down my face.

How charmed is my life this very minute.

How could anyone see this and not be a better human?

Alone I sat. Alone I bore witness. Why weren't there hordes and masses here to experience this?

I know why. People have to work. People have things to take care of. But this? It should still be a part of what is important. What should be an easier part of life to access.

In the dark I made my way back. The headlamp earned its cost tenfold. Back home I sat down in the quickly cooled night air and wrote. My best writing of this trip I thought.

I hadn't responded to many emails since leaving the campground with the lake. I had parked in the evenings in Walmart parking lots. I was tired and just went to bed each day. Now, I spent some time catching up. I hope folks didn't compare my responses but I ended up copying one in-depth and witty (in my opinion) response to one family member and pasted it as a response to quite a few emails.

I checked to see if any of my blog stories had responses. They did. People seemed to love 'meeting people' in my stories. Mason and Audrey were both getting some love from readers. I wasn't sure how to feel when my creative pieces received only a fraction of attention as my pieces about people and real life stories. It sometimes reminded me that no matter how good I felt something was, I can't predict how others will accept it. And I can't create anything better than what has already been created, and I end up just being the reporter.
Such is most attempts at creating something. I imagine.

Earlier while exploring the area I had come across a large fire pit. It was enormous. It was, according to the signage, to encourage strangers, campers, to gather. Everyone bring a little wood to add to the fire, a little story or music to add to the entertainment. As night came near I headed with wood in my backpack to the fire pit. No one was there. I sat for about twenty minutes. I felt pretty alone just sitting there and lugged the wood back to the van where I didn't feel alone.

The next evening I tried again. Again, no one else showed. I went back to the van and had my own little fire. The evening felt darker because of the awareness of other fires and people socializing to some degree.

The third night I returned to the large fire pit as night was turning dark. I had to step into and walk to the center of the fire pit, it was that large. There were remnants of a previous fire. I piled up the old pieces already there and some firewood already stacked to the side of the fire pit. I cleaned up the area around the burning center and got a fire going. I didn't have much wood to add, just the backpack full I brought. I stepped out of the pit and sat on one of the log built benches. Within ten minutes a couple walked up and added some wood to what I had left over and stacked next to the fire pit wall.

They said 'hi' and sat down. The woman spoke and said "we've come here for two nights and no one was ever here." I shared that this was my third night and it occurred to me that I didn't know who I was expecting to have the fire lit for me, us. Two men came up behind us and said "we had the same thought tonight".

Within thirty minutes there were 17 of us. Everyone brought wood but one woman who didn't have any wood.   But she had marshmallows and metal fire forks to roast them.   They were quite popular.

By midnight the fire was only embers but we all knew a few basic stories about some of us sitting together.

Fife (who's real name was Barney but everyone called him Fife after Barney from the Andy Griffith show) and his husband Evan are on a 4 week sabbatical to strengthen their marriage.   Both were feeling adrift and uncertain.   This time in the mountains and their extensive road trip was used to recommit themselves to their relationship, to one another.

Lisa and Lou were fast approaching retirement and considering life on the road.   For awhile at least.

They were doing test runs of life on the road to see if it was for them.

Greg was by himself, just out of a long term relationship. He wanted time to evaluate his goals, his own behaviors and he just wanted peace. It sounded as if fighting and noise had taken its toll on him.

Tori, Mike and George were just out for an extended weekend of drinking and eating campfire cooked food.

I couldn't remember everyone's names. I couldn't hear some of the names as they were spoken softly across a vast expanse over a fire. There were some who just seemed content to sit around and listen, not adding much to the conversation.

We tried to get a sing along but everyone seemed a little hesitant to belt out their true voices. That alone made the gathering feel almost forced, to me. So we sat around and spoke softly, or sat silently. It was a pleasant evening. But I didn't feel a connection to the people. Or the moment.

Though I wanted that, to feel connected, I couldn't make it happen. I didn't find it here, not this evening. Not in the few days I was here and with the few interactions I had. I found it in the morning talks with Audrey over cups of tea. I found it with Mason and Emmy sitting at a picnic table at a gas station. But on this mountain I felt more comfort watching the sunset alone than sitting around a campfire with others. It wasn't them. It was me. And I knew it. I just didn't know why. Maybe it's as simple as we can't feel that connection with everyone. I was okay with that.

It seemed hit and miss on where I might find it.

Some people I met and there was an instant understanding and connection. We were meant to interact for some reason.

Though the views here were worth staying for, I left in the morning. I knew I was just passing through this stop. I stayed longer than I should have. No. I stayed for the beauty of the mountains and the world. That was enough.

I did feel drained. Not really sure why. The energy of the place, or lack there of?

IV.

As I drove into the valley I knew I better make some plans. I pulled into the first store I found in the first small town I entered. A small but well stocked grocery store. It seemed to have everything anyone could need without the overwhelmingness of the big box stores that carried everything you didn't need as well. I restocked and carried everything to the van. As I was putting things away I opened windows and doors to keep the fresh air moving through. I saw through my open door a man and woman sitting on top of a picnic table in the park that ran along side the store. A dog lay on the ground. They were sitting next to one another but talking as if they were both looking at someone across from them. It took a minute of staring at them to realize they were facing a camera on a tripod. The dog was lying next to the tripod.

I went back to putting my groceries and toiletries away. I made a pb&j sandwich and sat down at the table to eat as someone knocked on yellow door's entrance.

I found the picnic-table-sitting-couple standing there. The woman, girl, had the largest brown eyes behind thick glasses with long brown hair pulled into a pony tail. She smiled and said "hi I'm Mia, this is my boyfriend Garrett. Do you live in this?" She looked up at me with those big eyes and innocent expression and I felt like she was more child than adult. Garrett smiled and did a little hand-wave 'hi'. He was much taller then Mia, lean, tan, his hair was also long and pulled back. There was a kindness emanating from them both. I don't know why I thought that. But I did. Strongly.

"Yes, for now."

"We're homesteaders, we saw your van and I thought immediately you might be a van-lifer. Do you like it? How long have you been doing it?" Mia's energy was infectious though Garrett seemed to stay at an even keel and just watch her with what appeared to be adoration. Though she was nearly bouncing when she spoke, Garret remained steady.

I offered them something to drink and a pb&j, they accepted the offer. I made extra sandwiches and pulled some pops from the fridge. Mia led us back to the picnic table. Their dog, Scamper, followed them to my van, and back again without making a sound. Over the next hour I learned about them. They are both 23 years old. They've known each other since the first day of kindergarten. On the last day of their senior year Garrett told Mia he'd had a crush on her since that first day they met in Kindergarten. He didn't want to ruin school years by dating, not dating, and taking a chance they couldn't be friends.

They were very good friends all those years. Mia was impressed by his ability to wait for her for 12 years. She felt they were very close all those years and had had no idea. She was also kind of jealous of his patience and foresight. From that last day of high school until today they haven't been apart.

Neither wanted to go to college but both were avid learners, readers and adventurers. Only they'd never been more than a few hundred miles from where they were born. They were a different kind of adventurer. They were living to discover new things about life is how they explained it.

Mia sat casually leaning into Garret who looked happier, and more comfortable, the closer Mia was to him. They are so young. But in a flash I saw them like this as an older couple. It's as if I knew they were a forever kind of couple. The kind, if you believe in 'other lives', they would always find one another.

They were living on Garrett's grandpa's property. It has been in the family for many generations. They've been there since one month after graduation. They had both been working locally but developing the property to be as off-grid and self-sustainable as possible. Mia was the last to quit her job in town, just last week, because they were now able to make enough to not work away from home.

In addition to the jobs they had been working, and working on the homestead they had created a Youtube channel to document their journey. That's what I had witnessed earlier when I saw them talking to the camera. They were working on a new video post. They were also doing work online. Mia did scheduling for a medical facility and Garrett was doing work for a credit card company.

There was a mutual admiration and fascination between all of us for the life choices and life style we were all experiencing.

Mia and Garrett started to tell me about all they had been working on when she sat up straight, so suddenly, it startled me. "Why don't you come see? You can park your van there and stay as long as you like!" She looked to Garrett for confirmation. He added with a smile "I think you'll enjoy it."

On the spot without giving it any thought I agreed. Mia stood and Garrett followed. "Okay, we only come in town for supplies about once a month and we haven't done our shopping and errands yet. You can follow us when we leave. In about two hours?" I told them I would be ready.

I sat down inside with my computer to email and post a quick update to my morning and what has transpired. When I left the mountain this morning I was feeling quite bland and possibly on the verge of being depressed. Now I felt a new energy, a resurgence, to see another life and place and people.

I sent brother an email with the what/where of my plans. Not because I felt any concern but I had promised him I would.

I had no idea how long before I would be back in town so I went back in the store and stocked up with more of my 'normal' goods and some additional treats to share with Mia and Garrett.

By the time Mia and Garrett were back at my door with Scamper I was ready and excited to go.

It took well over half an hour to get to their home. The drive to their home was dream like. The closer I believed us to be getting the more colorful the world seemed to become. When I pulled in behind them and realized we were there I knew it was a different world. I was already creating opinions. The first being how did they even leave here 12 times a year for grocery shopping. This place is simply-astounding.

The first thing, everything, about this place to notice is everything is growing. Even the far earthen wall of mountain behind the home appears to be growing out of the earth as it reaches up. I was holding my breath as I stepped on to the frame of the van doorway and stood above the door as I opened it and stepped up on the seat to see as much as I could see. Every where I turned my head…

I got back into the van to pull it where Mia and Garrett were pointing from their truck, further up the lane. They pulled the truck up close to the cabin. I waited until they got out and followed their directions on where to park. There were other buildings scattered around. Everything was so picturesque I didn't want the van to disrupt the view of any of it. Mia directed me to turn the van so the side door, yellow door, would be visible. I was parked long ways between some of the buildings, but in complete view.

Before they even took the supplies out of the truck Mia and Garrett helped me set up the van, its outside furniture, awning and moved some of their multitude of flower pots around the van to make it more a part of the place.

We all stood back and admired it. I turned to them to offer help carrying their supplies in. We all went to the truck and grabbed a box or bags. I followed them into the cabin.

All it took to feel at ease and comfortable (even more than I already was) was to step up on the porch and over the threshold. The cabin was everything and more. I had stepped back in time with a modern twist. Mia was as eager to show me their world as I was to see it. But I insisted on helping carry everything in first. The last thing we took out of the truck was a large cooler. We carried it into the kitchen and they insisted everything would be find until we got back to it.

Mia spun in the large living/kitchen/dining area. There were windows in every wall of the house. Everything was bright. Joy lived here. Windows were open. Curtains blowing softly. Fresh vegetables lay on the table.

Simplicity shines here. The wood walls and floor were the color of clear honey. One wall looked like it had been brushed ever so lightly with white, but it wasn't painted. The paint just highlighted the wood and lightened it even more.

Everything looked both old and new at the same time. Mia explained how the cabin had been on the land "forever" but not lived in for a very long time. Garrett's grandpa was the last to live here and he had moved to town many years ago. They had come in and scrubbed and power washed and sanded until the wood looked new again. Mia and Garrett made the curtains together out of bright and light gingham colors.

Table and chairs were refinished pieces they had found in one of the out buildings. Two chairs matched out of the 5 in the room. The couch was made of wood branches and covered with cushions they had made. The appliances appeared very 'retro' but weren't original to the home. The window frames were painted white. There was a story to everything in and about the home.

There was a freshness in appearance and feeling about the home.

In one wall of the kitchen was a doorway leading to a hallway behind the kitchen. Behind the kitchen the hallway led to more rooms on both sides of the hallway. The front of the cabin gave a deceiving appearance of being very small. There was a large bathroom with a clawfoot tub, a copper sink Mia proudly announced she had made. Behind the bathroom was an office with laptop computers, a desk top computer, printers, cameras and file cabinets. It was the most surprising thing about the home. It wasn't large, but very well organized and where a large part of their income was created and generated from they explained. Behind the office was a room being set up as a guest room which I was welcome to use but I declined. Another room was used to store canned foods and had a large utility sink and a wringer washer-functional and what they used for their laundry. I was welcome to use that as well. One more room was their 'power room'. Batteries and panels that outlined the electrical wiring and usage of the home from solar and wind power. They were still on grid because they had not yet made the final move to be completely off grid. The home had been on-grid since grandpa had lived there. They had been making the efforts to get off grid since they started working on the home. They were close. Because of the mountain behind them they had added wind power with a small windmill, and solar.

At the end of the hallway was a back door that led to another covered porch similar to the front porch. Paradise was growing back here. Flowers and vegetables and aromatic winds. It was so beautiful it almost didn't look real. Mia and Garrett were looking at me looking at their world. I turned to them with a complete appreciation for what they have done.

"Isn't it beautiful?" Exclaimed Mia. She actually clapped her hands together. She intensified the feeling. Garrett was looking at Mia, his expression of love intensified everything.

I was standing in another world.

They walked me through the 'back yard'. It felt like an enclosed and safe space. A wall of rock began where the yard ended, far behind the house, and appeared from that point to go straight up. If you looked from another angle further from the house you could see the slope of the wall. As we walked through the garden I discovered the reason and detailed planning of the yard. It was more than beautiful it was functional.

Flowers and vegetables that thrived in medium sun lived back here (because of the rock wall they lost evening sun). This is where the broccoli, Brussel sprouts, cabbage, carrots, kale, peas, potatoes and more were planted. Among the vegetables were flowers that would benefit and/or protect the vegetables. Herbs too. It was so much information that I didn't know I needed or cared about until Mia started showing me and explaining.

But while pointing out cilantro as a flower (who knew?) She stood up and said I could learn all of this later, let's see the rest of the house and property. Garrett and I followed along happily like we were on a leash tied to her energy. On the far side of the house were the clothes lines, with lavender planted the length of the house, and some rosemary.

Mia walked up to a towel hanging on a clothes line and buried her face in it. She lifted her face out and nodded her head to the next hanging towel. I planted my face in the towel and felt like I had dived into a wind swept lavender towel with a hint of rosemary. I had. It was wonderful.

We went back inside through the front door and they took me upstairs. It was one large room. They said it used to be three rooms, they changed that. There was a large bed they had made and a quilt they had made together on top. One wall had barn door sliding doors and hid a closet the width of the room. The back of the closet still had a window overlooking the backyard. It was painted and curtained just like the other windows.

The room was so simple. Airy and comfortable. Mia led us downstairs and outside to the out-buildings and "little barns". The original and largest barn had fallen in years ago. When Garrett and Mia moved here they went through all of the buildings, salvaging and organizing what was there and could be used. From day one they had started drawing (in a 3 ring spiral notebook) the plans for their home.

The buildings were as well planned as the home. There was a little barn for pigs. They hoped to get cows but had not managed to make that happen yet. The pigs were for them and their families. The smell wasn't great when I walked in but it didn't take long to get used to it. The pen for the pigs opened up behind the little barn. There were also goats, chickens, rabbits and more food growing in the 'side pasture'. Corn, beans, cantaloupe and watermelon, tomatoes and peppers.

It occurred to me that I knew more about these people in the 5 1/2 hours I've known them then some people I've known for years.

While we walked through the buildings, only two were left to be re-purposed, they explained their daily schedules. Up until about 5 months ago they both worked in town, Garrett stopped working off of the property first. Now, thanks to the internet, things were changing. Their Youtube channel was starting to make them some money, their food was coming mostly from their land now. They were making some money selling some foods at the farmer's market. Their online jobs. They had multiple, if small, income streams.

Suddenly Mia stopped talking and moving. Garrett and I stopped, almost uncertain what to do. Mia's appearance was deceiving. This girl-woman was a take charge and easily followable leader. She took Garrett's hand. "How about we all go finish setting up and putting our things away, I'll start dinner and we'll get the animals taken care of, then we'll set over dinner and talk some more."

"Can I help with dinner?"

"Not tonight. You're our guest."
"But feel free to come and go from the house, follow us while we do chores, whatever." It was Garrett's longest comment since I met him. We walked back towards the house, me splitting off to go to the van. In the van I did a little better job of organizing the

extra supplies, piling some of them in the passenger seat in the cab.

I set up my computer and was pleased to see I had cell phone and data, though later they connected me to their wifi as well. Brother had written back that he hoped I was safe in my crazy adventure and thanks for letting him know where I was (though he could also find me by my phone, another safety guard he insisted on me having). To give Mia and Garrett time to themselves I pulled up Youtube and found their channel. I went to their very first video. They looked young now, in the video they looked like they were ten years old.

They had a small, old camper they had parked at this property. The difference between now and then on the property was striking. Garrett had fixed up the camper his senior year of high school anticipating moving out here and working 'the farm' as they called it. The bonus was Mia coming with him.

That first video was full of excitement for their plans and future. The same excitement I saw and felt today. They were sitting on the front porch of the cabin before any work had started on it. The video shows the land and the buildings. Though unkempt and overgrown the outline of pasture and gardens was still visible.

I got caught up in watching videos of them. It was addicting watching them work, see mistakes made and addressed with patience (at such young ages!). It was mesmerizing to see the property take shape. Friends and family made appearances in the videos when they came to help or share celebrations and holidays. Grandpa, who owned the farm, was a frequent visitor. Before I knew it Mia was sticking her head in the doorway and saying "hey there".

I looked up from her smiling face on the screen to her smiling face in the doorway. "I found your videos".

She came in and looked over my shoulder "yeah?" She looked at the screen. "Now that was some time ago! We sure have worked our tails off." She crossed her arms while looking at the screen. I closed the computer and looked at her. Jealous, I think. "Well come on, let's eat!" I followed her to the house.

We sat down to homemade bread and rabbit stew. Mia apologized for dinner being leftovers. There was no need to apologize for such a flavorful meal. After dinner I insisted on helping with the cleanup, which took very little time. We went out to the front porch where Scamper was lying on the porch in anticipation of whatever dogs anticipate. We enjoyed the breeze, the aromas and the conversation.

I learned more about them. They learned more about me. I shared how I felt I was jealous of them. Jealous that they knew what they wanted at such an early age and worked so hard to achieve it. Garrett spoke up, softly and said "jealousy isn't what you're feeling". He smiled kindly. "If you were jealous you wouldn't be sittin' here sharing this day with us." Mia smiled in agreement. "If you're okay with me saying" he looked at me for permission to go on, a question on his face. I smiled my answer to him. "Okay then. I think you're a seeker. You have something out there to discover. You don't know what it is yet. And maybe it's more than one thing. I don't think you're jealous at all. I think you appreciate what we're doing and it calls to you for it to be appreciated. We're part of *your* journey" he smiled "and honored to be".

I thought for a moment in the comfortable silence. "Well, that's certainly a better perspective."

Mia added "and while we were driving home after meeting you? I found your blog and was reading it to Garrett. So we know a little more about you too." She winked at me. "We decided while we were reading that you're a seeker."

We wound down the night and went our separate ways. I spent another hour or more writing about this little paradise before getting ready for bed. I couldn't fall asleep easily. My mind wandered over the feeling of disconnect I was experiencing this morning at the top of the mountain. To a feeling of belonging and excitement, at the foot of the mountain. I was excited and looking forward to learning more about this life and these people.

I eventually drifted to sleep and dreamt about lavender scented pillows.

I woke thinking it would be after 9 am. It was just after 5:30 am and light enough to be midday. I smiled. I could get used to this. I slipped on a t-shirt and some shorts, and my hiking boots which would have to suffice as work boots. I made some tea and sat out on the bench to greet the sun. I just made it. I don't think I could ever take for granted this fresh and flowered air. The sun was teasing the eyes. The breeze tickling my ears.

What a way to start the day.

It felt safe here. A mountain behind my back propping me up and keeping guard. Mountains in the distance, like sentinels. A world at peace around me as people worked hard to provide for their family and others. I heard something in the chicken building. I walked over to find Mia collecting eggs. She smiled like she was expecting me. She put me right to work collecting. She showed me how to collect the eggs and explained while we worked that they do this twice a day. They don't want eggs sitting around and getting cracked by the chickens. They will eat them. And if they get used to that they will break them and eat them more. As we collected I learned more about eggs that I never knew. Like, don't wash them with water unless they're really dirty, and then use them right away. Washing them makes them more porous which makes it easier for bacteria to grow. Eggs don't need refrigerated but once you do refrigerate them , keep them cold.

The day was non-stop from there on out. Animals (and people) need fed. Plans for a greenhouse needed figuring so supplies could be planned for. Another garden was being laid out. In addition to what they grew for themselves and the farmer's market Mia and Garrett were also growing vegetables and giving it to families in need. To all of the families who accepted the free vegetables they also offered (but did not expect or require) to teach and help any family start their own garden. They would help them break ground, show them how to care for the ground and make it better for growing, if they needed help getting seeds they gave them seeds. They were pleasantly surprised at how many families accepted this offer.

We worked on the building they were turning into a school of sorts. They were continually learning and willing to share what they knew. They wanted to have a space dedicated to working with others. That was always in the back of their minds and part of everything they were working towards.

Every day was both the same (chores) and different as Mia and Garrett and I learned about something new to implement or make better. They absorbed me into their lives so quickly and them to mine. They taught me, I taught them, we researched things together. I learned about online tutoring, sponsors, transcribing, social media incomes and all of the different resources they tapped into to add to their income stream. Some were very small streams. But added together and with their physical farm and work they were creating a sustainable life right where they were.

The adventure of their lives was not stagnate because they stayed in one place. It was intensified by what they sought out and brought to it. And what they put out into the world.

Not a day went by that others didn't show up to ask questions, to teach, or be part of the world Mia and Garrett were creating. Garrett's grandpa, a quiet man, often came out to help and to spend time with Garrett. It was a common sight to see them working together, leaning on a fence talking or walking from one part of the farm to another while working.

They were building a stronger community by being active within it.

Some days I was calve deep in dirt and manure and two hours later sitting at a computer looking up how to make your own tea out of various plants.

We were outside in sun and shine, heat and bugs. Or when it was pouring down rain on our heads and there was no point in trying to stay dry. It was a freeing sensation to work in the rain because the work needed done and rain wasn't a deterrent.

Getting dirty felt good.

Getting clean again felt good.

The first time I washed my clothes in the wringer washer, hung them in the sun and wind, then put them on fresh with the smell of the world on them-I knew doing laundry like this would be a requisite to any life I built from here on out.

I fit in so well with Mia and Garrett that it sometimes caught me off guard when I thought of moving on. And that usually only happened when I was responding to inquiries from friends and family. One evening after chores were completed and I had made dinner for the three of us, we sat together on the porch. My skin had a fresh and hot feel from being in the sun all day. I was tanned and loving the muscle soreness at the end of a good day.

We had been working in the new garden with some of the families who had come out to help and learn. The day was incredible. People working hard without complaining and with a common goal. Often I would look from my task at hand to the world around me. The feeling I have here is similar to only one other place. I didn't want to leave there and I am developing a struggle knowing I have to leave here.

In three short and fast passing weeks I developed a passion for this place and what these people are doing. For being so young I learned so much from them. They were the epitome of inclusiveness and compassion. I want to be more like them.

Brother had been emailing, he seemed to be enjoying what I wrote about the place and the people. He asked if I ever thought I overstayed my welcome. I didn't think so. But now I couldn't help but deal with that pestering and intrusive thought when it snuck in on my quiet and reflective moments. Or when I sat here at the end of a great day and we were winding down in silence. It didn't get a chance to grow too much because Mia or Garrett, or one of the visitors would be calling to me, including me. Needing me.

My friends Hannah and Ealga wanted to come here. To experience what I was loving so much.

Leo wanted me to go there. Where he and Pilar are, I suspect, to tell them more about 'here'.

I looked at the tired and happy faces sitting with me. My hand was lying casually and lazily on Scamper's back. "You know, I'll have to leave soon."

It did not feel good to say out loud. I also didn't want to be watching them and see relief on their faces. Not that I expected it or thought it but we all have at least a smidge of doubt. Mia looked from me to Garrett and back at me "you *don't* have to leave". She stressed the 'don't'.

"I know I don't but I do. I mean, I do have other places to go."

"But you'll come back, right?" Her question felt good. I believed they enjoyed me being here. Truthfully I did not want to leave. I was more called to stay, at this moment, then I was to leave. But I knew, soon enough, 'I will' leave.

"I hope you know how much we enjoy you being here. You belong here."

"I know how much I appreciate being here Garrett."

"But you don't feel you can stay?" Garrett taking the lead in a conversation was surreal.

"It's not that at all. But I do have places to go."

While we spoke I feared Mia getting upset, which was not like her. She didn't disappoint. She sat back and smiled. "You'll be back Bronagh". I smiled at her just accepting that. She believed I would return, so leaving wasn't an issue. I felt less stressed having said it out loud now. And, because I believed Mia. Without knowing it. I did believe it.

I didn't leave right away. It was more than five weeks since my arrival, five weeks of feeding animals, cleaning up after animals, collecting eggs, learning about growing things, and myself, growing closer to the people who the farm attracted and nurtured. Growing closer to the place and the land. I was able to go to some of the other families homes and help start gardens. I even canned some tomatoes into tomato sauce, green beans, apple sauce and beets.   Though I refused the offer of beets when they were handed to me. No. Thanks anyway.

I had 'gone to town' with Mia and Garrett for monthly supplies and purchased what I needed. It felt odd driving away from the farm and a relief on returning. We had finished the greenhouse. We planted some mid-summer vegetables to be harvested late fall. I was surprised to learn some vegetables could grow into winter. The greenhouse was going to increase their growing potential and teaching potential. The building they wanted to turn into a school needed a lot of work for what they wanted to do but we had it cleaned out. We laid out the plans to expand it. The long term plans included more solar power, some computers inside, areas to build (carpentry) and teach and learn more about power sources (solar, water, wind).

I was grateful to be witness from my bench one evening to a wonderful moment for Mia and Garrett. We had finished chores and dinner and gone our separate ways. I was enjoying a cup of Mia's homemade chamomile tea blend when I saw

Garrett's grandpa, Henry, pull in the lane and park behind the truck. He threw up a hand and a smile at me as he walked into the house. Not twenty minutes later he walked out, smiling, threw up another salute, and left. After he was gone for a bit Mia come out and made her way to the bench and sat next to me.

"Grandpa just left."

"I saw. He was here kind of late."

"Yeah. He wanted to give us something."

"Oh." Her tone didn't indicate any worries. I just enjoyed that our homes, their cabin and my van, were so connected. And comfortable for all of us.

"Yeah. The deed."

It took me a second. "The deed? To *here???*"

She could only grin.

"He knows. This place belongs to you both."

"He put both our names on it. Not just Garrett's".

"Oh Mia". I couldn't say anything else. It was just so right. So wonderful for them.

"You know, we hoped to get part of it, or an opportunity to buy part of it. We never expected him to just give it to us out right."

She didn't need to scream or jump up and down for me to know her gratitude and excitement. I know what she and Garrett put into this ground and what they took out of it to share. I knew what this meant.

Mia stood up. "I just wanted to let you know."
"Thank you." I watcher her walk back. Home.

The next morning after chores the three of us walked the farm. Not all of it but a good bit of it. By now I had seen all of their videos and had worked on nearly every part of the farm. This walk was full, if possible, of even more excitement, plans and energy. Ideas were created with every step it seemed.

I hadn't told them yet but I would be leaving in the morning. This walk with these fine people was bitter sweet. We walked for miles and made our way back to the garden behind the house. Mia said "you're leaving aren't you?"

"Tomorrow morning." She and Garrett both nodded. We went into the house and sat down for some lunch together. We had all been gifted some peaches from one of the families who had gone peach picking earlier in the week. We had made pies and canned pie filling and jam. We mostly ate lunch so we could eat fresh peach pie.

The day moved by us quickly. A good day of work and friendship. We worked together and separately as we each had different jobs to get done. In the evening after chores they asked me to go for a ride with them. We all piled in the truck, Garrett driving, Mia in the middle and me in shot-gun. Garrett pulled out of the lane and turned left. Less than half a mile up the road he turned right into what used to be a lane to another home. Now it was the memory of a lane and home. The truck bounced a little but not too bad. He stopped the truck and Garrett got out, my cue to get out as well. Mia slid out after Garrett. They walked to the front of the truck, Mia climbed up on the hood and sat there. She patted the spot next to her so I climbed up and sat. Garrett sat against the bumper and leaned into Mia. It was so peaceful. The sun wasn't dipping behind the mountain behind us, yet. So the sun was dancing across the tops of the wild flowers. It was an old homestead. Long gone buildings were still outlined in the bare spaces before us.

"We own this now".

"I'm excited to see what you do next". We spoke forward, to the world, without feeling a need to turn to one another.

Mia turned to me. "You'll be back. You'll be back."

"I know I will."

Garrett turned to look up at us both. "We know you have to leave. But we also know you'll be back.

It may not be soon. But you will." Mia nodded. "And when you do this place will be waiting for you."

Smiling came so easy here. It was a solid form of our communication. We smiled 'yes', or 'got it' or 'thanks'. Mia started laughing. She knew I was grateful for the extended welcome. "No Bronagh" she put her hand out "this place-it's waiting for you to come back."

I looked out past where her hand extended. To the spot where someone's house once stood. Where she was telling me I could be. Stay. Live.

We have spent most of every waking moment together for the past five weeks. During that time it never felt repetitive or 'too much'. Working. Sweating. Laughing. Sharing meals. Learning from others, teaching others. I feel, believe, we have become very close. Intimate-in a world where intimacy is often misdefined. To be wanted in a world of disconnection was beyond what I had ever expected to find. To stop in a parking lot, meet two people and their dog and become part of a community of people all seeking the same things. To belong. To be wanted. To be a benefit to the community. How to describe that feeling when someone seeks you out...when a friend calls or comes over because they were thinking of you, when you receive a job offer for a job you weren't looking for because they wanted you specifically for a job, when someone says 'live here because you belong here' when you didn't know where you belonged.

In that moment I knew the definition of friendship. Truth. Faith. Intimacy.

We remained where we were. I looked from where Mia had indicated-back to their faces. And smiled.

I think a tear fell as well.

They smiled their acknowledgement of my thanks.

"Come." Said Garrett as he stood up and we slid off of the hood. We joined him to talk around the area where a house once stood and people lived.

I imagined living here. It made me smile. I stood looking out over the world, imagining the world that the people who would have lived here must have seen.

Eventually I turned to see Mia and Garrett standing by the truck. I joined them and we drove back. When we got out of the truck I turned to go to the van and Mia stopped her steps toward the house to remind me to come to the house in the morning. We'll have breakfast together.

In the van I put away laundry I had brought in earlier from the clothesline. I washed the few dishes and put things out to make tea in the morning. I wrote a quick blog but did not share what Mia and Garrett had done for me.

My time with Mia and Garrett had given me so much to write about. Their work, their goals, the mountains, the people, the growing and giving. And these stories garnered so much dialogue. I always encouraged people to visit their blogs and videos. It confirmed and validated what I believed. People want connections.

I slept well. I woke knowing-almost exactly-the time. I guessed 5:43 a.m and it was 5:41 a.m. when I checked. I'd been doing this guessing game since my second morning here. I was getting pretty good at it. I turned on the kettle for my tea. I thought my heart would be heavier, but after last night there was something about leaving that was easier. Maybe knowing there is a place and people to come back to that I believed I was beneficial to.

I dunno.

I made my tea and made my bed. I went out to head to the chicken building (we didn't call it a coop) but heard Mia calling me from the house. I walked over to find Mia and Garrett standing on the porch. They moved to one side and the door came into view.

A yellow door.

They had painted their front door to look just like another 'yellow door'.

Mia was nearly vibrating and clapping her hands. I looked from them to the door and back. "We stayed up so late painting it. And got up to finish it. Don't touch it, it's still wet".

"You guys…." It was touching. Funny. Endearing.

They came down the steps. "We can't go in this door. We still have to get the eggs and feed." Life here is amazing.

We did the chores then went to the house for breakfast. We had eggs, bacon, pancakes with homemade syrup brought to us from one of the families, toast from homemade bread, tea. And talk.

I helped with the cleanup. Garrett disappeared for a minute and came back with a large wicker basket. "This is for you". It held canned foods from all of the families. Jars of Mia's homemade tea. A small supply of fresh vegetables. Garrett had made the basket and I was informed of exactly where it would fit in the van and I needed to use it for laundry instead of shoving clothes into bags. There were mini loaves of five different kinds of bread. Home made candy. A small jar of lavender and rosemary that Mia had made so I could smell the yard when I was missing them. And a bundle tied together with a ribbon of cards and notes. Lots of them.

"I'll carry this to the van for you." Garrett picked up the basket and went out the back door with me and Mia following. The van had not been moved since I parked it here over 5 weeks ago. As they helped to set up they helped to tear it back down. We packed the bench, the rug, moved the flower pots and made sure everything was secure. We checked the tires and aired them up. I had run the van routinely but not moved it. I had driven their truck and small farm tractors. It felt weird getting behind the wheel again. For many reasons.

I backed the van out, turned it and got out.

It was the quietest moment between the three of us. At the same time we all spoke the same words..." thank you". We all smiled. Though not a hugging kind of bunch, we did. I got in the van.

And left.

V.

As I passed the yellow door of the cabin it was difficult to keep the pressure on the gas pedal. I knew I had to go on. Not that I wanted to leave. I knew I had to see more.

It felt odd. Not working in the sun. I thought back over the last five weeks, as I often would. Work. Yes. It was dirty sometimes. Harder at times than other times. Though we called it 'work' it didn't have the same feeling as other jobs I'd had. Previously I went to work because I 'had to'. These last five weeks were work because we wanted to. We looked forward to it. We thrived on what we were all doing. That was thanks to Mia and Garrett for what they created and shared with me and the others. This is how 'work' should feel. Some days we only stopped because the sun went down or our bodies gave out. The desire to do what we were doing never stopped.

I observed the land changing as I drove. Though it took a long time it eventually changed from foothills to rolling hills, to flat countryside. The road sometimes crossed the water that went from creek size to river size. I passed through an intersection that passed as a town, the first of many. I was aiming for a campground that would take 6 to 8 hours to drive to depending on how often I stopped.

I arrived 5 hours and 48 minutes after leaving. It was raining. I paid for one night, backed in and opened the windows just a crack. Made dinner from the gifts in the wicker basket. Fresh canned green beans, chunk of homemade sour dough bread, fresh made applesauce. After cleaning up from dinner I sat in my chair, propped my feet up on the bed and read my cards. I was cry-laughing at most of them. At the very bottom of the bundle was a pale yellow envelope with a plain pale yellow card inside. On the card was written "Come home when you're ready". Signed by Mia and Garrett.

I sat with the card in my hand for some time. The smile remained on my heart. When my legs got stiff I sat up straight, pulled out the computer and checked emails and comments. Five weeks of working every day got my body in good shape for moving. It was difficult to sit still but it was still raining and I didn't know what was around me to go check out. I stood at the kitchen counter, emptied the wicker basket and turned it upside down and made a standing desk.

I was surprised at the number of comments expressing surprise that I had left Mia and Garrett's. Many had been reading and commenting with me for a couple of years. They thought I would stay there.

As I stood alone in the van I couldn't help but think about what they were doing back at the farm. I was a little surprised as well. So I set my sites on seeing things I needed and wanted to see.

It occurred to me not for the first time that all of the beautiful places I wanted to see didn't necessarily end up being the best part of the travel. Good/ great views vs. good/great people. One always made the other better.

I opened my maps, the folders of travels, and pulled out the list of places to see. I closed my eyes and circled my hand around and around and then dropped it on the list.

I opened my eyes to my finger on Glacier National Park.

Nice.

I googled the drive time. From point A (here) to point B (there) was 33 driving hours. It would take a lot longer than 33 hours on back roads.

I mapped out a drive and places I could stay. While I was doing that Mia sent me a text, a picture of the pumpkins. I sent her a picture I took of the computer showing Cobalt Lake. I sent an email to those tracking my travels with the newest destination.

I looked around the little van. It hadn't felt little in such a long time. I closed the windows but stood looking out. It wasn't little to sleep in. It was comfortable, cozy. But it was enormous when it was parked at the farm and life was lived outside.

There was no work to do. No one was around to talk with. I settled in for the evening and read until I fell asleep. Over tea in the morning I researched hikes at Glacier National Park and looked for suggestions of what to bring and how to be prepared. I've hiked a good bit but not alone with bears.

I was back on the road before 10 a.m. I skirted the edge of Tennessee by-passing Nashville but thoroughly enjoying the country. 'Skirting the edge' of Tennessee still required a few hundred miles. I spent the night in a Kentucky Walmart parking lot. It was the first time I was told to leave. Around 5 a.m. there was a knock on the driver's side door. By the time I managed to peek out and see it was a police officer he had knocked, louder each time, three times. I opened yellow door and the side door of the van. He had stepped back and had his hand on his holster. Scared the crap out of me. When I slid the door of the van back and he saw the 'house wall' with the yellow door he smiled. But he still had to tell me to leave. His curiosity got the better of him and he came in after asking if he could see the van. He ended up sitting with me for over forty minutes talking about the van and life on the road. His name was Liam. He loved the adventure of it all and was very apologetic but the store manager insisted that I leave. I assured him it was not a problem. We talked about how my trip was now being directed to GNP and I showed him the pictures of it on the computer. I saw his eyes take in the views. I think he fell in love. He told me to take my time getting ready he would sit in his cruiser and write his report by the van so the manager didn't come out and say anything. I told him I would be ready in 15 minutes or less. When I climbed into the driver's seat, dressed, with a tumbler of iced coffee and my bed made I rolled down my window to thank him. He walked over to the door.

"Hey, do you have time for breakfast?" That took me by surprise. "And can I call my wife to join us?" That made me smile. He had me follow him to a small diner that opened at 5 a.m. for the farmers and factory workers and closes at noon after selling lunches to go. We sat in a small booth. Liam's wife Lizzie joined us. From the kitchen. They owned the diner.

Over breakfast of eggs, hash browns and coffee they peppered me with questions about the van, the set up, the plans, the life. They asked how I got up the nerve to make such a big change in life. The best answer I could come up with was "I didn't have the nerve to live life the way I'd been living it." When I decided to 'go' I found an energy I didn't know I'd had. Working jobs that didn't fulfill me drained me of energy. Once I made the decision to change things they were 'easier' to do. Easier to go knowing I was going toward something. Going to work had a new energy because it was going to pay for the changes I wanted to make.

They wouldn't let me pay for breakfast and Lizzy gave me a box of their homemade cinnamon rolls. They wished me safe travels and sent me on my way. They were working hard to change their lives. Though they didn't have a desire to change everything about their lives, they did want to add to it.

I had forgotten the soreness of all day driving. After I left the diner I made it through Illinois and well into Missouri. I stopped at an old fashioned general store. It was originally built in the 1800's and was still used as a store today. I went in to ask directions to a campsite and ended up talking for 50 minutes and receiving an invitation to park overnight at the store and hook up to their water hose and their electric.

I actually spent two nights because when I woke up in the morning the store owner told me they had fabulous wineries (I had no idea) and took me around to some. I don't think I remembered them all. Doris, the store owner, at one point called her mom to join us. Or drive us. But she did both. I don't remember the wineries exactly but I remember having a great day. I had to sleep another night in the store parking lot to sober up. When I left the next morning it was with two bottles of Missouri's finest. And it was pretty fine.

As I drove through middle North America it constantly ran through my head-repeatedly-how better this world would be if everyone traveled it more. Met more people. Saw the mountains, the plains, the little towns, the big lakes, the bigger oceans, the little ponds. If we encouraged kids to travel as much as (or more) as we pushed college on them. If vacations were as valued by the world as working over-time was. If we just met each other in one another's own worlds. Our country. Other countries. My belief is that it would be a better world.

That's what I thought as I drove. I painted a pretty good picture in my head of the value of meeting people, sharing our worlds, and the impact that would have on relations. And understanding. Nationally and internationally.

Unfortunately I don't run the world. But I got through most of Kansas and into Nebraska creating this idea. I'd write about it at night and wait for the world to take notice and tell me the brilliance of it. Most comments were along the lines of 'that's a great idea' and let it go at that. Some responses, as in real life, felt like shrugs when I read them. Others were thoughtful and considerate. So much for my brilliance. Even the shrugs were messages I paid attention to.

In South Dakota I decided to go off course a little bit and head to the Badlands for a short visit. What an education I found. I didn't consider myself a stupid person but the older I got the more I owned my ignorance. Because I knew very little. I was okay with the not knowing but I was not okay with the not learning so I could know more. The internet afforded me a lot of education. I preferred books and found a used book store on my way to the campsite. I picked up books written by the locals (always look in local owned bookstores for those). The internet was a great segue to find information that peaked my curiosity while I read.

I enjoyed learning about history but couldn't stand the idea of a history textbook. Give me a book about the life of someone and the history of their time and I could get lost in it. Enough so, that sometimes when I put a book down I was briefly shocked to find myself in my time period.

It was both fascinating and disturbing to read the history of this (any) place. One history would read blandly about the changes in the land development and the discovery and study of the fossils and how the parks were developed. Another history would read of slaughter and the destruction (genocide) of the Native Americans.

When I first crossed into South Dakota I stayed a couple of nights in a campground with no amenities. It was a good test for being off-grid and being mindful of my supplies. I had stopped before getting to the Badlands and stocked up and geared up a little better. Being on the farm had acclimated me to doing with less 'inside'. Being outside felt better and more productive.

My 'inside' activities were basically sleeping or reading. While reading about the Badlands, those readings led me to Native American reading, those readings led me to reading about worldwide genocide, all these readings led me to some very long hikes to get some of the horror of humanity out of my head.

There were too many times and too many stories-world wide-where people tried to wipe out entire cultures. I did an internet search. I was dumbstruck. The initial search suggested genocide could have been what happened to the Neanderthals. That's just a hypothesis. But from that time period forward, in my limited knowledge of geography, it appears that man-globally-has a history of trying to wipe out people who are different than the party attempting to wipe out others. Equally shocking was the discovery (to me) that same-culture genocide was horrifyingly frequent-based in politics and social divides-scares me that we haven't gotten smarter about that.

Globally.

This was numbing. Disturbing. And not great fodder for travel thoughts. But there it was. It was a rabbit hole to hell of information.

One afternoon I returned to camp and found that almost every site had become occupied. There were people everywhere. The volleyball pit was full of players and spectators. All of the picnic tables seemed to have become laden with coolers and bags. Tents, pop-up campers and RV's of every size and age dotted the landscape.

When I had left to take a hike it was quiet, barely morning. I don't remember seeing any tents. Maybe that one RV was there. My site was fairly primitive, no hookups. A bathroom and shower house were nearby. The site was clean. I had a little patio I parked right next to and put my rug on. A fire ring and picnic table filled the small site. I was content with the site.

I've adapted well to being alone easier then re-adapting to people. But I can do it. Sometimes it's more of a shock than others. Like returning from a hike where I saw no living anything but plants, to a boisterous group of bipeds roaming about. I made lunch and made the tomorrow decision to start out early enough to catch the sun breaking and watch it transform the rocks into a painted version of itself.

I checked my emails and found Pilar had written. Normally it was Leo who would write for both of them. She repeated Leo's on-going invitation, and asked if I planned to head their way to let them know and commented on my travels. She thanked me for writing about my travels because it had prompted them both to make plans. She looks forward to seeing me.

The noise outside called to me. But I couldn't make out what the noise was saying. I headed out and walked to the volleyball pit. I never knew there was so much interest in volleyball. I hung around and was smiled at and hello'd at a good bit but couldn't really connect with anyone. I spent the rest of the day people watching. I cooked a great stew over the fire. I wrote some. I even made a few short phone calls, something I prefer not to do. I wasn't a fan of the phone, for calls or texts.

I was excited to see the world in the early morning hours. I packed my backpack with food, water, chair and notebook. After the stew was done I ate an early dinner and watched peoples mill around me. It was relaxing to watch them. There was no stress in being expected to join. There were lots of waves and smiles.

I read, entirely, Eli Wiesel's "Night". It was the second time I had read it. What a difficult read. What a necessary read.

As night fell I ate more stew. Drank a cup of Mia's chamomile tea and found myself standing in stillness. I didn't relight the fire when it went out. So absorbed was I in "Night" that I realized no matter how I tried I could not fully grasp the horror of that experience. I felt both guilty for not being able to and relieved that I didn't have to. Which circled me back to guilt.

Even with the help of the tea I did not sleep well. I woke long before the alarm. After filling my thermos with fresh, hot tea I added it to the backpack and headed out into the darkness. I was able to hike further than I had anticipated. I found a spot highly recommended on the internet for sunrise viewing. I set up my chair, put my notebook in my lap and poured myself a cup of tea.

Initially I sat and thought about humanity. Collectively and historically-as a whole-we often look like a shit show. I had to force myself to change the direction of my thoughts. I started to mentally list people of character and the benefit of them to us. I thought about gratitudes. I was lucky enough to be sitting in this place when the earth's brown and grey tones gradually welcomed the kiss of the sun. I forgot to set up the camera with time lapse. I didn't care and I wasn't going to move now.

I sat.

I watched.

I continued, prompted by this view, to think of all of the wonderful and kind things I personally know about other people.

Slowly and yet still too fast my eyes saw the world transform. How ironic. I went from the darkness to the light simply while sitting here. The change was both profound and simple. Yet transforming. On so many levels.

How can I put into words here what my eyes bore witness to? The black outline of the solid earth-meeting the grey-no-lite-blue-air of the atmosphere. Wait. Coming up from behind the dark earth-an orange hue-a yellow hue-push into the veil of pale blue. Spreading out. Not crowding the blue-joining it. So very soon a brilliance-center stage where I gaze-comes that brightness. It looks to forcefully, gracefully, dip into earth as it bursts into sky. It's a deceptive vision. But so powerful it does appear.

And the world is exposed. The beauty of the cloak of night lays bare the truth of day as it slips away.

What appeared in silhouette dark, shows the depths of rocks in wave and color. Exposed once again.

I realized I was leaning forward. As the sun topped the line of earth I relaxed back into my camp chair. I heard a scuff behind me and turned slightly to see a young woman-20 years old or so-also sitting in a short camp chair about 15 feet from me.

She smiled. I smiled and looked forward again. Words didn't feel necessary, or appropriate.

I sat for some time in the brightness of the rising sun. Breakfast was a protein bar from the bag. The tea was perfect. Without warning the world seemed to come to life in other ways. Though I had set myself and my gear off of the actual walking trail it was still next to it. Suddenly it felt like there were people every where. Walking right by me. Within inches.

Magic show-done.

I waited until the small groups passing by-passed. I packed up. The young girl sitting behind me was also packing up. When I stepped onto the trail and walked, she fell into step next to me.

"Thank you" she said and stuck her hand out. I shook it.

"For what?"

"For sitting in silence with me."

"You're welcome." She didn't need to explain it. I fully understood.

"I'm Amelia".

"I'm Bronagh".

We discovered we are in the same campground. She was quite somber, this Amelia. Not sullen. Just very earnest. She didn't waste words but I learned enough. She was friendly just not boisterous. Her demeanor and appearance presented a confident young woman. But I couldn't get much more than that. We parted ways at the trail head of the campgrounds.

I hadn't made any plans for how long to stay. I decided on one more night. I rode my bike to the office to make sure I could and to pay. I was pleasantly surprised that I could, the park seemed pretty full. I checked my route to Glacier National Park and took inventory of what to get before I got there. I had a better-than-breakfast-was-lunch. Sat in my chair outside to read and woke up two hours later.

An evening hike seemed to be just the thing to wind down my short stay. This time I made sure to pack my camera and little tripod and my headlamp. I chose a different hike. I wanted to see the layered walls of stone. The hike out was hotter then this morning's hike and the sweat felt like it was soaking me. I passed quite a few hikers coming 'back'. I hiked a short way until I sat facing the walls of stone. Where the earth built itself up layer by layer. Then the winds and rains shaped it to make the mind wonder.

I set up my chair. I was very early. I set up the camera. I sat. And I stared. What did this earth look like before it built up? Or wait, was the earth that high and this is from erosion? Something to research. Who witnessed it? Were prehistoric beings awed by visions like this? Or were they too focused on survival. If they noticed were they capable of poetic thoughts? Contemplations? This is how my brain works.

The wind and the sun were drying me out. I hope a thermos of ice coffee and a large water bottle will get me through sunset.

I had brought along "How I Learned to Ride The Bicycle" by Frances E. Willard. Not a large book. It piqued my interest at the last bookstore I stopped in. I was captivated by the first page. I heard a crunch and turned to see Amelia approaching. She smiled, which gave her a radiant look. She indicated a space next to me to sit. I said "please do". I held my book, ready to read if she wanted to sit in silence again.

She asked what I was reading. I told her and she said "oh, Frances Willard." Seriously. She knew this. She laughed. I didn't even have to ask her to explain how she knew about this woman from the 1800's who was a suffragist, politician and advocate for woman. She learned how to ride a bicycle then wrote about it. She told me. "One day I was helping my grandma go through some old family things. She handed me a small calendar diary from the early 1900's and said 'this was in the hands of your great-great-grandfather. For an entire year." She settled her chair and her backpack and she told me the rest of the story.

"When she put it in my hands I went through every page. He was very concise with his words. He would write 'ofc' for 'office' and miles he traveled for work for that day. But every few pages he wrote something-brief-and more personal." She pulled a sandwich out and offered me half. I pulled my own sandwich out and we did a mini-sandwich salute. "On one page he drew a bell and wrote the word 'wedding'. It was his wedding day to my great-great-grandma." We ate for a minute.

"Grandma gave me the diary. Every place he wrote about driving to I looked up on the internet. Every person's name he wrote about. I looked up. Her name, Frances Willard, was written. I'm not sure why he wrote it. He also wrote the name of a hall he went to, when he wrote her name. But it couldn't have been to see her. She was dead by then. Maybe it was a play or speech about her. The hall didn't exist any more."

Amelia shrugged. "So I read her book." She nodded at the book now lying on my backpack.

"Did you like it?"

"Loved it." We sat staring at the earth. Not each other. "You're in that van. With the yellow door?"

"I am."

"You live in that?"

"For now."

"Why?" Such a simple question. But so much harder to answer simply.

"Well. Partly because I enjoy the travel. Partly because I find it difficult to sit still. Partly because I don't know what to do with my life."

Without missing a beat she said "at your age?" I burst out laughing. She was serious but smiled at my laugh. "Yes, at my age".

"So, while I'm wondering, now, what to do with my life. You're *still* thinking it at your age?" She didn't need to stress the 'still' so adamantly.

"Sure. I headed right into the work force during and after school without considering there may be other ways to live. Though all the while thinking 'is this all there is to it?'"

"Same. Now. I mean. There are traditional things I want. A home. Family." She stopped talking. Maybe she wasn't comfortable talking to a stranger. We sat quietly for a few minutes. "But I don't want that to be 'all' it is. Life, I mean. It sounds selfish."

"What sounds selfish?"

"Not wanting to lose something. Myself? Possibilities and opportunities? Because I don't want a traditional life to get the traditional things. But. I want the traditional things."

"There are a lot of ways to 'do' life. There aren't any parameters on how you have to do it." I pulled up my backpack and pulled out my notebook and pen. I wrote Mia and Garrett's blog and YouTube names and handed it to her. "You know, I waited too long and learned way later than I should have to start doing things that felt good. I'm not sure why we think life has to be a drudgery or parts of it have to be-to earn joy in life." She took the paper I extended to her. "Here are some folks doing it different. I learned a lot from them." She took it, read it, took a wallet from her backpack and put it inside.

"Thanks".

"You're welcome."

The colors of the sky were starting to change. I reached over and turned the camera on to capture it in a time lapse. We enjoyed the slow change. Quietly we watched. I could see others dotted around the trails. Watching. Though Amelia wasn't talking her presence was loud. I had no way of knowing her thoughts but I felt as if she was experiencing some heavy thinking.

When the sun went down we again packed up and took the short hike back. Together. She stopped in the campgrounds before splitting off from me. "I just wanted to thank you." Her smile was genuinely mood altering, up-lifting. "I think sometimes it's just validating to hear someone else say the very things you believe. Or wonder about. I have a difficult time talking like this to my friends. So…thank you." I gave her one of my yellow cards.

"Any time." We went our own ways. I didn't have much to do to get ready for my morning departure. After I was done I built a small fire and sat outside with a glass of iced tea. Life in this campground was now fairly busy. It was wonderful to see so many people loving this life. There was more foot traffic, bicycle traffic and occasional moped or electric bike traffic than motor vehicles. Each night I had seen camp fires, I could smell bacon in the morning. Outdoor dining at its finest all day.

A group of people walked by. Amelia was among them. She waved 'hi', as did the rest. I couldn't help but wonder about her life. What kind of decisions she'll make. What she will find and create. Who will benefit from her being in their lives.

When I left in the morning I didn't see another soul along the way out of the campgrounds. None awake anyway. I saw a few sleeping in chairs around fire pits.

VI.

I took a couple of days to drive through Montana. I could have meandered for much longer. I enjoyed the towns and being stopped out in the middle of nowhere by trains. No hurries. No stress. It crossed my mind often how grateful I was for the ability to do this. When I told Leo that, in one of my emails, he reminded me how hard I had worked to make it happen. I did have to remind myself this didn't happen easily. The two years of working two jobs after returning from Ireland wasn't easy. Not to mention all the years of working prior to Ireland, and then changing my entire life to make that happen. Which made me all the more grateful for the ability and willingness to make it happen. The roads across this world are beautiful. Though I've only been to limited 'parts' of this world-these roads make me want to see more of it. Some stops for gas or food ended with long conversations with curious, interesting and/or entertaining people. Some stops were quick, business was dealt with and that was all. People were busy, overwhelmed or uninterested in communicating beyond what was necessary. They still intrigued me.

The ones who were curt or courteous but busy, I wondered about them. What is in their lives? Stress? Sadness? Even good things can occupy our thoughts and keep us distracted.

This part of the country I was driving through didn't seem to have a lot of people. And it was beautiful.

My phone rang. It shocked me enough to physically startle me. Other than using the phone to call stores or businesses to ask questions I mostly avoided phone calls. I answered by pushing the button on the steering wheel and Mia's voice filled the van. I smiled. "Hiya Bronagh!" With an echo of "hey Bronagh!" From Garrett in the background. One of the many nice things about this phone call, it got me through an hour of driving without me noticing an hour flew by. Mia caught me up on the progress of the farm, the families who were learning with 'us' and the school building update.

She also let me know 'Amelia of the campgrounds' contacted them. Mia was also becoming fast friends with Hannah and Ealga (via blogs and internet) from Ireland. I found it exhilarating that people were connecting with one another. Perhaps via modern means, but in a very human and real way.

Mia and Garrett had decided to build a stand at the 'bottom of the road'. Just another way to sell vegetables and other things that families were making. Including breads and jellies. One of the teenagers was taking fallen limbs from trees on the mountain and carving hiking sticks. The Farmer's Market was only one day a week and seasonal. If this roadside stand works they might keep it open more days and for a longer season.

It felt as if I was sitting at the table in the cabin with the breeze blowing in.

Missing a place is hard.

Missing people is harder.

It was nice that saying 'goodbye' didn't feel like a goodbye.

I had been approaching the mountains, passing from what felt like flat lands forever, to now mountains looming everywhere. The views were, at times, more than my brain could fully absorb. Sometimes it felt like I was looking at a painting.

I stopped at the first pullover to get out and stretch. I sucked in my breath as I stood at the foot of the art created by glaciers. I wasn't sure how I would ever be able to drive without stopping every two minutes to stare. I stepped inside and made a tuna sandwich then sat and just stared. At one point I realized I still had the sandwich in my hand. I ate it mindlessly sitting there. When I went to take a bite and didn't have a sandwich in my hand I wasn't aware I had been eating it. I wasn't even in the park proper yet.

The traffic was lighter than I had anticipated so I took my time. Pulling off at many of the designated areas for photo-ops and staring. Staring is an under-appreciated method of meditation.

Eventually I made it to my campground of choice inside the park that had bicycle access to the nearby park 'village' and visitor center. It had amenities but I chose a site without hookups because I was prepared. And it was cheaper. It was relaxing to set up home and know I wasn't packing up to leave in the morning. It was close enough to ride my bike to the 'village' to enjoy what it had to offer. The campgrounds were closer to empty then they were to being full but that would change quickly. With my rug out, slide door open-exposing yellow door-bench set out, chair set up by the fire pit, I was fairly done. I rode my bike to the village and familiarized myself with the area. People were milling about with smiles and hellos. I discovered another bike trail from the village and took my time pedaling its length and back. It felt good to be physical. I also discovered biking was permitted on almost all of the park roads with precautions and only a few restrictions.

Back at the van I checked my hiking gear, packing it for expected excursions. I spent the rest of the evening responding to emails and connecting virtually with people-friends-from what seemed around the world.

Before sunset I hiked to the nearby lake to catch some stunning views. I wasn't disappointed. I hadn't consciously made a plan to center my travels on seeing nature and creation but that seems to be where I am called to go. Man made things don't call to me like this does.

The clouds had started to roll in before I left for my evening hike. They looked 'heavy' and loomed grey. But they had a backdrop of a white bank of clouds behind them. Not for the first time I had a strong desire to be able to paint the visions created above and around me. Visions that changed with nearly every step. Though the clouds were heavy-the sun was low enough and approaching the level of the water-to shine under the clouds and over the water. It was a spectacular view.

I was not the only one who had this idea. I reached the banks of the lake and set up my chair. People were talking softly. I was greeted with 'hello's and 'hey there''s as if I was expected.

I sat.

I watched.

Talking ceased. Sighs increased.

The sun's last rays seemed to stretch-with effort-to reach us on the banks. To bathe us in a brightness that reminded us of something, it was telling us something, it was comforting us.

The sun created a path to us. Then took it back as it pulled itself down below and past the horizon. Using the distant and low range land between the mountains that valley'd us-to hide behind and make its silent exit.

Good night sun.

No one moved immediately. Who wanted to walk away from that?

Gradually though, as humans do, talk resumed. Though hushed. Though peaceful. Though happy.

I remained, as those who chose to move away respected the reverie of those not moving.

How long I sat was only evident in the tears I felt on my shirt when I again became aware of my own existence. Again I was reminded of the connection between nature and our own emotions. How does that happen?

I hadn't felt the tears. Only the emotion.

I slept well that night.

Breakfast was cooked over an open fire. My tea had an extra flavor of 'smokey' added to its blend. While cleaning up my breakfast mess I saw a woman riding her bike-suddenly jump off-and look at her back tire. She took off her helmet to display a mop of spiky silver hair. She hung her helmet on her handle bar and turned the bike to walk away. Flat tire. I stepped out of the van. "Hey".

She smiled up at me "hey".

"Flat?"

"Yeah". I motioned her to the back of the van and opened my 'garage'. She wheeled over.

"I'm Bronagh".

"Thanks Bronagh, I'm Maggie". She busied herself taking the bike cooler off of the back rack and deftly flipping the bike upside down to rest on the handle bars and seat.

I had a small air compressor, spare tubes for me but she had already pulled her own tube out of the bike cooler. I admired how the cooler was part tool box and part food cooler.

"I'm just up the road. Figured it would be easier to change at camp with my compressor instead of using up an air cartridge". She had several air cartridges and an inflator. But I'd have done the same thing.

"I have a similar set up" she nodded her head to my van. "Do you like it?"

"I'm loving it so far". I had the compressor on and building pressure. I can change and fix a flat but she made it appear easier than I ever experienced. She had the tire off, tube out, found the hole, checked the tire and found a partial screw head embedded in the tire. She pulled the screw out, rolled up the bad tube and put it in the tool box end of the cooler for later repairs, while we waited on the compressor. "I'm still pretty new to it all" I followed up kind of lamely while I watched her.

"I've been on the road for two years. Love it." She took the compressor hose when it kicked off and put a little air into the tube. She placed the tube in the tire and rim, aired it up and got it seated again. I watched quietly while she worked. It was soothing. Competent hands working is a joy to watch. When she was happy with it she put the wheel back on the bike while I packed up the compressor and closed up the garage. I retrieved some hand wipes for her to clean her hands. She was grateful. "I see you have a bike. Want to ride?"

"Sure". I got a water bottle, put my pack on my back, secured the van and put on my helmet.

"I've been here a couple of weeks. Riding is nice when traffic isn't crazy. You just get here?"

"Yes. Yesterday." We hopped on the bikes. "I'll let you lead where to go." We left. Freedom. And we pedaled. It was easy. The pedaling and the company. Maggie was more than a few years older than me. She married very young. Her children were adults now. Just as their children reached adulthood she and her husband started talking about divorce. They hadn't decided-committed-to divorce but she felt it would have happened. Sadly, he died while on a hunting and fishing trip with his friends from work. They had an emotional, but good, talk before he left. He had said "let's not make any decisions. I'll go on this trip, you spend some time doing what you want, then we'll decide together". They had hugged and agreed to do just that. They were very easy going with one another. They just weren't emotionally together.

They didn't get the chance to make any decision. It was made for them. They had never told the children, so she never told them after he died.

We rode along quietly. I wasn't sure what to say. She glanced over her shoulder at me with an understanding smile. We had ridden through the village and onto a new-to-me road.

After his death and later her retirement she felt life closing in. And fast. She had no desire to do much and that depressed her. As we rode Maggie would interrupt her story and point out magnificent views and pepper the conversation with tidbits about the park she had learned since being here. Next thing I knew we were pedaling along a low stone wall. It didn't come near as high as my knee. The world on the other side of the wall seemed to disappear. But if you looked out the world picked up and shot out of the ground in magnificent snow dotted mountains. We rode through a short tunnel and parked our bikes on the other side of the tunnel. We stood looking past the barely there wall, drinking. I pulled some cookies from my bike bag and shared them with Maggie.

"I've monopolized our ride".

"I've enjoyed it". Whenever the world presents itself in stunning, undisturbed glory, words didn't seem necessary. Actually…they kind of feel obscene. We stood silently. We stared below us and out past and far beyond what we have come to expect in life. No walls. No power poles. No vehicles.

We got back on our bikes and rode back. Suddenly the road seemed to fill with traffic. Everyone seemed to be cautious. We saw bikers coming towards us on the other side of the road. People were every where. It wasn't the casual ride out we had initially enjoyed. On our return Maggie said she was making fajitas if I would like to join her.. I gladly accepted. She told me her campsite number and told me to give her about an hour as she left me at my van.

In the van I grabbed the last mini loaf from my Mia/Garret basket. Zucchini bread. It would be a nice treat to take to lunch. I posted some pictures I took on the bike ride. Even being here it was difficult to believe such beauty existed.

I heard something that pulled me back outside. Lower than I would have expected was a helicopter flying into the park.   I didn't know they had helicopter tours.

Within the hour I was riding to Maggie's camp site. She was easy enough to find.   I saw some people walking away from her van as I came around the bend. She was walking back towards her van. Her fire was burning in the fire ring and she had an outside kitchen set up under an awning.   Things smelled good. I parked the bike next to hers.   I brought the zucchini bread offering. She smiled "I love baked goodness."

"Zucchini bread".

"Wonderful!"

"Can I help?"   She nodded to a basket with dinnerware. "Sure, set us up." I set the picnic table, already covered with a vinyl cloth. I liked how it was fitted to the table, like a fitted bed sheet for a picnic table. And wipe-able. No need to take it off and on. I grabbed my water bottle from the bike, it held some ice cold tea. I offered her a glass before I started drinking from it. She pulled a beer out from behind the lunch fixings in front of her.

"Ah." I helped carry the tortilla, pan of hot veggies and chicken, salsa, sour cream, chips, lettuce, tomatoes, jalapeños, etc… to the table. We sat down to a mini-feast.

As I sat down she asked "do you mind if I say grace?" I smiled "not at all". Maggie laid her arms on the table, either side of her plate, bowed her head. I mimicked this, the prayer was a simple but sincere gratitude for the food and the company. She looked up, I said "amen" and we started building our fajitas.

"Did you see the helicopter?"

"I did."

"A hiker died". I stopped building my fajita and looked at her. "I don't know yet if it was some kind of accident or something medical, like a heart attack."

I sat quietly for a minute. Maggie continued creating her fajita. She started to lift it for a bite and lowered it a little. "You okay?"

"Yeah. Just sometimes…I'm so grateful for my experiences right now. I forget the realities of life."

"I get it. This type of living appears 'free' and unencumbered. But at the same time it's very insulated."

"Exactly".

"I can't tell you the last time I watched the news. If I catch the news at all it's usually only when I'm driving and have the radio on. Or I purposely pull it up on the computer. And that's rare."

"When I first realized how little I knew I started to feel guilty." She raised an eyebrow at me while she chewed. "I quickly got over that." That elicited a grin, and a lift of her fajita.

"So what's your story Bronagh? How did you come to be here?" I told her over our lunch, then a beer.

Then another bike ride to the village for ice cream. She was interested in reading my blog stories. I usually start my story from the decision, the point in my life where I decided to change everything. And go experience living on an island. That is a story all unto itself.

But Maggie is very astute. She asked about life before that decision. I raised an eye, grinned and shrugged. "That's just it Maggie, there isn't much to tell to that point". We had stopped at my campsite and were still straddling the bikes.

She squinted, just a little, in that contemplation way people do. "I get it. Some stories you, we, don't share because you think they aren't as exciting, or valuable, or interesting. Here's something though, those stories always have value." She winked at me and before I could respond she said she was heading off. There would be cards played at her site tonight if I wanted to join. And she pedaled away. I rolled my bike to the van and opened the van to get fresh air going through.

Maggie seemed to think I believed my life, to a certain point, wasn't valued. By me. It was. It is. I'm just not there any more. And some stories, we don't want to share.

I had noticed many people using hammocks at their campsites. I seldom had a feeling of strong 'wants' anymore. But man I wanted one of those hammocks right now to lay in and take a nap. Outside. In this air. Instead I laid a throw on top of my picnic table and slept.

I woke up to campground noises. Muffled but pleasant sounds. Soft music coming from all directions. Everyone was considerate of their camping neighbors. I also woke up stiff and sore. I went in the van and on the fridge was a small magnetic whiteboard where I made a grocery list and a 'to do' list. I added 'hammock' to the list.

I brought the computer out and sat at the picnic table. I wanted to write Mia and Garrett and was happy to see they had sent me numerous emails full of pictures and activities. I was touched, as always, by their compassion and desire to help others. They had met with the local churches to see how everyone could work together to make their free lunch/meals better for the individuals in need. They were going to meet with other local farmers and growers about donating fresh vegetables to the meals. In this way they could also increase their already happy way of teaching others about gardening.

As I sat there I could hear someone pull in to the camp site on the other side of the van. I heard the now familiar sound of doors opening, closing, and a vehicle being maneuvered into place. Sounds like a good size RV. With my back to the van and the direction of the newly arrived camper I put on headphones and went through the emails.

I sent Mia some pictures from the day, pictures that I would't put on-line. I answered some of her questions and asked some of my own. I don't think I'd ever been as invested in people as I was with Mia, Garrett and the "families". By the time I finished with the emails, writing and doing some minimal researching about the area I was currently 'living in' I could hear the new neighbor's noises through and over my headphones. It sounds like a full blown party had begun already.

I really had a strong urge for pasta. I picked up the computer and went in the van, grabbed the last of my fresh spinach, a small onion, garlic, cherry tomatoes and feta cheese. I chopped what needed chopped and put it all in my largest pot. To avoid the party revelry I decided to cook inside instead of on the camp stove outside. I put the lid on and put it on the back burner. On the front and only-other-burner I put a pot of water on. I plopped a big dollop of olive oil in the water and let it come to a boil. As the items in the big pot cooked I mashed the the tomatoes a little bit and mixed it all. But not so much as to lose the chunky texture. After the rotini (only pasta I had) cooked I drained it and mixed it in the large pot. This would be better baked but it was smelling incredibly good. I felt sluggish and didn't think I was up for cards at Maggie's. We had exchanged phone numbers and though I was not a fan of texting I sent her a text telling her I wouldn't be there for cards but hoped to catch up with her tomorrow.

Gradually I became aware of an almost rhythmic sound. It occurred to me, suddenly, it was rain. I had no idea it was on the way. I opened 'yellow door' and stuck my head out to do a quick scan, making sure there was nothing out there that shouldn't be getting wet. As I finished my 2 second scan the sky unleashed. I shut both of the doors but still had to mop up water that got in that quickly. I checked the windows, checked the pasta, and got ready to relax. It was darker than normal, lending to a very cozy atmosphere. The rain was pounding but soon it was just part of the atmosphere. I didn't hear it separately, it was part of the evening.

Once I was set up with some Youtube videos of other 'van lifers', I got a big bowl of pasta, a glass of wine, and commenced to an evening of rain serenaded-video-watching-pasta-eating-night. Ah. And the revelry that continued 'next door' even in the rain. Technically a storm since thunder had joined the party.

Pasta-very good.
Videos-fun and informative.
Storm-enjoyable.

New neighbors-celebrating something.

When I finally cleaned up and turned in for the night the neighbors were in full swing. Fortunately the rain dulled their noise 'enough'.

Then the rain stopped. Around 2 am. The neighbors did not. I'm not sure what time they did settle. From 2 am I was awake more than not. I allowed myself to get frustrated, which probably kept me awake longer than the noise did. I finally got up. Forced to do so by the inability to sleep. Even though the neighbors were wonderfully quiet by then. I heated some water and made a wonderful pour over coffee.

A long buried desire to retaliate was stirred this morning. To make noise and disturb them was briefly entertained. Admittedly it made me smile. But I didn't have the energy to create noise chaos. And I hoped other neighbors were now enjoying some quiet and sleep. Who knows...maybe they were celebrating something amazing, or relief from something terrible ending.

My brain and energy were sludge. I took a look outside, being on top of a mountain had benefits. The road and parking spot were paved so no mud. But everything was wet. Even with the coffee I couldn't muster enough energy to do anything. Fortunately the weather played along with me, remaining grey with periods of rain. Days like this, more about not having energy than the rain, made me very grateful for having put a bathroom in the van.

Maggie sent me a text to say she heard I had new neighbors. She included party favor emojis. I told her whatever she heard was not an exaggeration.

Even after drinking the large coffee I fell asleep. Waking up at almost noon. I felt like crap. It was raining. The only noise was rain. I looked outside, no surprise, some of the campers had left. Weather or noise related I wouldn't know.

Though I would gladly have held the party RV responsible for how I felt, I felt too bad for me to think it was only a lack of sleep. I took out my first aid kit, found my thermometer and was not surprised of my 102.6 temperature. I took some ibuprofen, made some tea, put honey in it for calories. I wasn't hungry but didn't want to deplete myself any more than I was feeling. I checked my texts and most could wait. Maggie had texted a few times so I sent her a message about my fever, my tea and I'm going back to sleep.

Fevered sleep. You never know what you're going to get. Complete-blackout-pass-out. Or dreams that bring you with them.

I traveled the world courtesy of that fever. I started by waking up in a cottage, on an island, with a raging storm. I stood there and smiled. So grateful to be back. Even while dreaming I knew I was dreaming. I drank tea from a familiar mug. I stood still and inhaled the aroma of burning turf. Slowly I turned, all the way, to make sure everything was the same. There, on the table, was the old typewriter. The 'kitchen' remained the same, there sat a partial loaf of bread. My rain jacket hung by the front door. I stood enjoying the sounds of the Irish storm, the smells of the cottage. I finished my tea and placed the mug on the table, next to the typewriter. After one last backward glance I slipped the rain jacket on and walked out into the storm. It felt shocking, electrifying and energizing. I walked without fear to one of the cliffs and took a giant step down to the ocean.

With great glee and surprise I walked across the ocean. I went through London but didn't dawdle. I made my way to Belgium. All the while telling myself to enjoy this because it wouldn't last, I would be waking up. I smiled until my jaws hurt. In Belgium I gave my coat to a young boy and told him to give it to his grandma. He said "okay" in English and I thanked him.

I was so glad to be walking through Belgium. The colors were stunning. I found myself thanking someone for a boat ride and found it odd that I couldn't remember the boat ride. But it made me happy none the less. I stepped out of Belgium and into Venice. How beautiful and such an unexpected trip. I felt the elation of the travel even though in my dream I knew it wasn't real. I found myself hungry. Someone handed me something to eat as I sat in the gondola but then I was splashed and I couldn't find the food.

I woke up. Looked at the ceiling above my bed fully expecting to see the skies above Venice. Can't deny it, I felt disappointment. I turned my head, surprised to see it was dark. One of my LED lights was on. I went to sit up, it took a lot of effort to make it all the way. A lot.

I was drenched in sweat. I closed my eyes and sat there to orient myself and take stock. When I opened my eyes I saw a covered dish, not mine, on the counter. I reached over and plucked the paper taped to it-off.

"Bronagh, please forgive me for coming in. I came to check on you a couple of times and you didn't answer my knocking. After 3rd time I tried the door, it was unlocked. You were OUT OF IT. Here's some soup. Just heat it up. Please LMK if you are awake and/or need anything. Maggie"

I touched the dish, still warm. I made myself swing around and put my legs over the bed. I had nothing. No energy.

The benefits of van life. I could reach the silverware. I pulled the dish close without lifting it. Couldn't have lifted it if I wanted to. I pushed the lid off and dipped the spoon in. Slowly I managed to get a bite, then another. Then rest a few seconds. Then another bite. It was chicken soup with large chunks of carrots and celery. It was obviously home made. And it was everything.

I looked around. My tea cup mug was on the shelf by the bed with a bottle of water. The tea mug was empty. The water was half empty. After a few more bites I found my phone in the bed and sent Maggie a text. The best I could.

"Awake. Barely. You are angel. Soup good. Talk later. Going sleep. God!"

The soup was helping. I sipped water. I heard music and wondered if my computer was playing something. Then it occurred to me, the neighbors. At least it was pleasant music to hear.

I dragged myself off of the bed. I was feeling chilled. I went from bed to chair. It took too much effort-more than I had-to tug the sheets off of the bed. But they needed off. I balled them up and shoved them down beside the chair. When I thought I could stand, I did. Surprisingly I didn't feel as weak when I stood up. I gathered some fresh clothes, t-shirt, shorts and a towel. I felt grungy. Put the kettle on to heat up water for more tea, took more ibuprofen and took a van shower. I didn't feel good doing it, and maybe it was only a mental boost, but I did feel better after. Though fully exhausted by the effort. The old clothes got shoved next to the chair with the dirty sheets. I don't care for disorder but to hell with it for right now.

I made more tea, put honey in again. I was grateful I wasn't sick to my stomach. I wasn't hungry but I didn't want to get dehydrated. I ate more soup and felt even more gratitude that the dish fit in my refrigerator so I didn't have to bother with putting leftovers in a smaller dish.

I pulled my other set of clean sheets from a cabinet and threw them on the bed. I gave myself another pass and didn't actually make the bed. I made a nest on the bed. After sitting up sipping on more tea I reached up and turned the light off. I set the computer to play some reruns and that's the last thing I remembered.

When I opened my eyes again it was to morning and a stinky van. And no fever. I couldn't have run a marathon but I did manage to get up, open windows and do some straightening and eat.

I had to take another shower. I hadn't stepped foot outside of the van since…before the rain. Yesterday? The day before?

Redressed again, with tea in hand I went outside. I was surprised to find everything dry. I walked around just to be moving. I stepped into the road. The party RV was gone. I don't recall if I ever even actually saw it. There were fewer campers around.

I went back to my outside chair and sat down. I really hoped the van aired out. Sick bodies do not create lovely aromas. I sent Maggie a text that I was up and out. It was nice to see her come into view with a smile and a sit down.

"Thank you so much."

"You were out of it. I felt like a crook breaking in when…" I waved that off. She grinned. "You were so far gone. Do you remember talking to me?"

"Did I? I have no recollection. God. What did I say?"

She laughed. "Nothing crazy. You could barely form words. I got you some water. Got you to drink some of it."

"I was too sick to know how sick I was."

"Yeah. I remember being alone, and sick. Even if you don't need anything there's a lot of comfort in someone knowing you're sick. And keeping an eye out for you."

I let that sink in. "Thanks Maggie. Even though I wasn't aware, I'm very grateful you broke in." She laughed with a snort. Which made me laugh. She caught me up with the party RV-ers. So many people complained that something was said to them.

They actually went around to apologize to those they could find outside. They weren't asked to leave, they left on their own for whatever reason.

We talked about how I was feeling. We had a quiet sit for a bit. At the same time we looked at one another and said "I'm ready to leave here". Another short laugh. I deferred to her. "I'm ready to go to Oregon. I've got some friends I plan on staying with for awhile."

"I was thinking of going along the Pacific Coast Highway. At least part of it."

"No pressure, but we could travel together for awhile if you like."

"That would be fantastic. I think I'll wait until tomorrow. Just to make sure I'm feeling okay." We made tentative plans based on how I feel in the morning.

I felt like writing. I wrote out the entire drama (not really since I was blacked out to any drama). The point of what I wrote came down to what Maggie said. About being alone when you're sick and there being comfort in someone knowing you are sick. And watching out for you. How many people exist without that basic comfort? It was a sobering thought.

I checked in with Mia and Garret. Rather. They checked in with me just minutes after I posted my blog. They were worried. I assured them I was fine. They gently reminded me I would always have someone watching over me.

As soon as I finished talking with them brother called. Another assurance that I was fine. Another reminder that he supported me but times like this made him wonder again about my safety.

The van needed a thorough cleaning so I took my time and put order and fresh air back into the van. All the doors were opened, fans kept running. I got laundry ready for the first laundromat I would come across when leaving. I didn't have full steam yet so breaks were taken often.

When I finished I walked to Maggie's and found her doing the same thing to her van. She showed me where she was heading via her mapped out trip on her phone. It was likely we would only convoy together for two, maybe three days. We both needed to do laundry and shop. Neither of us was in a hurry.

When she closed the app on her phone there was a picture of her and a man. I tapped the edge of her phone nearest me and said "husband?"

She looked at the picture and smiled, said "it is" paused, "was". She pivoted on the chair to look at me while she leaned into the chair. "I can't really talk like this with my kids or family. No one knew about our potential break up". She glanced at the phone as the picture went to black. "But I can't help, you know, wonder. What would our relationship be like now if he had lived?" I knew it was not meant for me to answer. So I listened.

"I was always grateful for him. Even when we talked about divorce. He was calm. Kind. Neither of us were hateful or angry. In all the time since his death I've wondered..were we just bored with each other?" She tapped the phone again to see his face. She turned it to me, I smiled. The faces in the picture were smiling. Appearing happy. Still, it wasn't for me to speak.

"Sometimes I let all kinds of scenarios play out in my head. Him returning from that trip and us getting divorced. Us not getting divorced and growing distant. Us not getting divorced and finding our happy again. But you know my favorite scenario?"

I raised my eyebrows. "Us getting divorced. Making independent decisions. I like to think I would have still done this" and raised her arms to encompass all around us, van, travel, exploring. "But, he and I, we would find one another again. I know. It's stupid. But I imagine running into him in a million different ways. Like…" her eyes lit up some. "We both did this" tipping her head back to the van "and we find ourselves parked next to each other. Totally unaware of what the other had been doing. We cookout. Drink. Laugh." She looked at me directly, with tears. "Maybe cry". She shrugged. Wiped her eyes. Dropped her head onto her propped up hand.

"Maybe I'm stupid Maggie, but it seems like maybe you are doing that". She tipped her head to look at me. "I mean, finding him. Again."
After a moments silence she smiled and said "maybe neither of us is stupid".

We left in the morning. We spent three days caravanning, stopping often to look at something, walk through a town and eat. During the drive I found myself going further north. Checking my maps I realized there was another highway along the coast in Washington and Oregon. I decided to add that to my PCH drive.

Maggie seemed to have changed, even in the very short time I knew her, since breaking her long held-in struggles about her husband, his death and her never to be answered questions. A little more subdued. It didn't change her readiness to smile but the smile itself seemed a little more somber. I was sad to part ways and though she was too I got the feeling she was ready to be alone again. She would take her time getting to her friend's place. Each night she sent me a brief text of her day. Oddly, my favorite time with her was when we sat outside of her van and she told me about her husband and her what-ifs, maybes and could-a-beens.

VII.

My first night without Maggie parked next door I had a call from Mason and Emmy. They wanted to tell me they were expecting a baby. I was touched that these people I spent a few hours with wanted to share this enormous joy with me. When we hung up I sat and looked at my van, parked in a Walmart parking lot and thanked this incredible life.

I slept well at Walmart. Waking to a sunny but cool day. I pulled up maps of the "PCH". I spontaneously decided I wanted to start at the most northern tip of the highway and make my way as far south as I felt the call/need/desire to go.

I was so focused on the PCH and then Highway 101 I didn't scout out much about Washington or Oregon. Knowing I would come back when my focus was on different discoveries. I don't know where the determination came from to start at the very most northern point, but it was there. I had zero knowledge of the coast and probably less knowledge of Oregon and Washington and California. I was adding 'to go' places on my computer lists by the dozens. Now, I wanted to get to the ocean. I wasn't looking for sandy beaches. I wanted rocks, cliffs, boulders, wind and foam topped power waves.

Driving to the tip of the 101 was my focus. I took as many non-direct and non-highway type roads as possible. I wrote about the day travels and the night wind-downs. Many people commented on my blog posts about all that I was missing by not stopping even more than I did. I was well aware I was not seeing all that could be seen and fast falling in love (again) with the new parts of this earth I had never seen before. I felt like I was heading somewhere. I had somewhere to go. Even though I didn't know what or where it was. I just enjoyed the getting there. Every day.

I slept in new places and only drove a maximum of 300 miles a day. And that was rare. I was finding it comforting and rewarding to be alone again. Though I spoke almost daily with Mia and Garret, had some video calls with Ireland, and responded to emails and texts, I was for the most part alone. I didn't, for the moment, need to rely on anyone. But

I knew they were out there. There was a certain kind of freedom to that.

By the time I was approaching Olympic National Park I was ready to stop for a couple of days. Without having done much planning or searching I found where to go to seek a camping site. The frugal part of me wanted to park somewhere free. The 'I want to see amazing things' wanted to park somewhere that I couldn't find anywhere else. The park campsites were fine, but, I wanted something that wasn't done by everyone else.

At my last store-stop before hitting the park I bought some canvas storage cubes and added a larger 'pantry' courtesy of the empty passenger seat. I knew I was over buying but I wanted to be prepared to stay some place if I came across an 'I'm called to stay here' kind of place. And the less shopping stops I had to make the better.

Every time I see some place stunning I think I've seen it all. Every time I think that I'm wrong. Though I was strongly focused on getting to the coast I didn't want to be oblivious to the road I was traveling to get there.   Literally.   I drove, appreciating the intense views.   When I needed to physically move I found parks and hikes. I didn't want to just move to get rid of van-ass.   I did take advantage of sites along the way.   I stopped usually once a day for a restaurant meal or coffee. The best food on the entire drive was from a food truck. All I got was a hamburger and French fries. But all that I got was locally grown, raised, baked and homemade.   Even the pickles were cucumbers grown by the food truck owner's grandma and pickled by his aunt.   I actually dreamed about that meal when I went to sleep that night.

I recommended that food truck to everyone.   Even to my friends in Ireland.

When I finally arrived at Olympic National Park I spent the first day hiking all the short trails I could find.   I hiked about ten miles that day but did 3 different trails.   The Hall of Mosses was like another world.   I was alone and didn't want to go so far I had to carry provisions.   Not to mention I didn't want to pay to carry in and camp in the wilderness.   I didn't think I would have the right gear for that. That night I was tired. My van was set up for the night and I sat outside with a diet Coke, a rare but so appreciated treat. I had a map of the park and maps of hikes. Over 180 hikes. I was not sure where to go. I wanted to see waterfalls. And trees. The giant trees. The trees that had in them the air of and breath of centuries ago. I waited until the fire died, I made sure to put it out completely, took some Tylenol and went to bed.

I spent three days hiking. My longest day was 16 miles, but again, they were made up of multiple smaller hikes. Oddly, or maybe not, the more I walked alone in the woods the more I wanted to be alone in the woods. Maybe it was because I knew this wouldn't be forever. Though I could see why people would want to disappear into this kind of world. I wasn't opposed to human contact I just didn't seek it out. I had conversations with random hikers and people at the campsite but I relished my time on the hike walking among something that had been here forever that we hadn't managed to destroy. It was refreshing and energizing to see people who appreciated the rugged reality of earth.

After the three days of hiking my feet were screaming with rebellion. I spent a day of lounging at my campsite and went to the park office to seek out alternative camping information and find out how to 'get around' the park to the other side. The park ranger asked me about my plans and took me to a map. You don't go 'through' this park. You actually do go around it. She spent a good deal of time with me, sharing the park's history and telling me about the Quinault Indian Nation and history. She was so passionate I asked her if she is Quinault. She smiled and said yes. Her pride was evident. I think my brain was as numb as my feet because I couldn't absorb half of what she was telling me. But I was fascinated by her and her passion. To see her expressions change as she spoke not just about her heritage but her passion for nature and the park itself.

She stopped speaking mid-sentence and apologized to me. I didn't know what she was apologizing for. I looked at her name badge, "Jae", she said I came to get assistance and she was keeping me. "Jae, you aren't keeping me from anything. You're why I'm here. I enjoy learning and discovering. I'm not in a hurry." She insisted on getting back on track with my questions. She asked more questions about my plans. She was intrigued. She went outside with me and had a tour of my van. Seeing how self contained I was she suggested some free campsites outside of the park that would be more 'on the way' to where I was heading. Highway 101 or "One". She suggested I do the 101 loop before heading south towards the PCH. She said I would not regret it. I offered her tea or pop. She declined but we leaned against the front of the van and talked longer. When we parted I was heading towards some camping along 101 and had decided to do the loop around the park.

While driving alone I sometimes pondered over the hundreds, thousands, of people I passed on the roads. Lives that I will never know about. Full, complex lives. I would be in their physical circle for the smallest fraction of a second. All of these worlds passing, crossing, circling, never to connect. Then there are those micro-connections. Clerks in stores, calling someone by phone for assistance, speaking 'hello' to strangers as we pass by-our aura's converging-but nothing remains to connect us. It blew my mind anew every time I paid attention to the actuality of lives being lived that I have no knowledge of.

Then. Come the lives I do have knowledge of. Equally as surprising. To know of them but not *know* their full experience.

I'm a thinker of these things.

Jae had directed me to some private owned camping. If I didn't plan on using utilities of any kind I could stay for free. When I arrived I found the spot she told me about that she liked best. I backed the van in and when I opened the back doors I was pretty pleased with the framed picture of a river rushing over rocks with trees fancying up the edge of the frame. A tree framed picture. It was lush. Probably the first time I ever used the word 'lush' in my life. Before I even set up camp in this lushness I walked the road I had driven in on, a little past where I parked, to see if others were around. I walked down to the river finding places to sit near the rush of it. I'd sit for a minute or ten and move on to the next place.

My desire to physically move was strong.

When I made my way back to the van I set it up. Full set up. Sliding open the side door so yellow door was visible, opened yellow door for air in the van, put out the bench from the garage, set up the little table and put out my chair. Then I made coffee. I moved my chair to the edge of the river. I was a good 10-15 feet above the river in my little world.

Sitting and wondering. How many times can I sit alone and be content to be alone. I pray there is no limit, but something unthought was poking my subconscious. I felt it. But chose to ignore it. Instead I settled my thoughts into the sounds and the views. When my coffee cup was empty I went back to the van and made a pb&j, a tall glass of iced coffee out of what was left in the pot and went back to sit on the edge above that river. The sound was intensified by the arch of trees and the echo created by the rocks.

The almost rhythmic sound lulled me into yesterdays. I finished eating and sat back as the river pulled memories from over-packed and stacked corners. I smiled through childhood flashes, grimaced through some of the teen years. And let life just flow rapidly with the river, bouncing all over the place, appropriately just like the water crashing into the rocks or flowing rapidly by. Too fast. Nothing to slow down the rush. You can't stop that rush once it starts and gains momentum. As I sat staring blankly at the river, with my memories as much a part of the view as the river, a floaty entered my vision. A round, made to look like a pink donut, rubber, floaty. I watched it bounce and pass me by without so much as a how-do-you-do and float/ bounce out of sight.

Now I want a donut.

I took an eye-opening look around me. No one was with me. No one knew where I was. Generally speaking, yes, brother, Mia, Garret, Leo and Pillar knew. Even my friends in Ireland knew generally where I was. But no one knew exactly what was going on. Or where I sat. Or really, why. In the moment I was feeling two very polar opposite feelings. One, was to stay right where I am. The river's hypnotic, crash, rush, yet soothing rush pulled at me to remain sitting.   Enjoy the mesmerizing lull. I'm comfortable. Not challenged. Appreciative. Two, was to contact everyone I knew. Leave. Connect. Be part of other's worlds. Find challenge.   Each of these thoughts was powerfully demanding and calling me.   Neither stronger than the other. I was content being alone, alone when I wanted to be. I made myself get up, walk back to the van and get my phone and computer.   I returned to the river and sat there with my fingers flying over the keyboard. Writing emails to people I had possibly neglected, or not heard from after the last time I reached out to them. I spent well over an hour doing that.

I moved back from the river because of the noise and spent almost two hours on the phone calling people. It felt good. Laughing with people. Falling into comfortable and long used speech patterns "I know, right?!", "that's crazy", "no way!". The best of it though, was the laughter. I hung up with 2% power left on my phone battery. A full bladder. An empty stomach.   After recharging all 3 I realized how good I felt. Very good. Being alone was my choice right now. It didn't mean I chose loneliness. I was feeling grateful for the people in my life who were happy to hear from me.

As I puttered around the van I had a random but powerful thought. *This* is selfish. I stood up straight from checking my water supply and looked out, then stepped out of the van. I looked around me and saw everything. And nothing. Such beauty. But facing me in this glorious place was the truth. Standing right there in front of me. I could acknowledge it or completely disregard it. I sat on the bench and faced it.

I go so I don't have to be fully myself.

Those odd little thoughts that make themselves known. Some of them are trying to tell us, me, something. I have spent the better part of the last years of my life working very hard to make time to be alone. Because being alone I only have to be partially me. The one I have to be around others, is free, of having to be. The partial me is fulfilled by calm, peace, no drama. The other part, the part with people, when it is good, it fulfills the need to challenge myself, to be charitable, to be helpful.

Is it, was it, a great life living on an incredibly vivacious island? Yes. Is it a great life traveling solo in a van doing what I want when I want? Yes.

Is it easy? No. I worked very hard to make this happen. No one gave me this life. No one gave me the means to have this life.

Where is this coming from? No one. Just me. I zeroed in on the scenery. The greenery. It grew up. It hung down. It was above me and below me. I could get the sense of being closed off from the world. In all manner of interpretation.

What am I doing?
Why am I doing it?
Where is it taking me?

I felt frustration at what is prodding and prompting these thoughts. Selfish. The word kept tapping my brain. Demanding to be addressed. As I looked over the outside of the van to make ready for night I tried to defend the selfish thought by denying it. By the time I went inside and made a cup of ginger and turmeric tea I decided, yes, I am being selfish. Is that wrong?

I put on my 'pajamas', sat in my chair with my feet propped up and pulled the computer to my lap to write.

I am being selfish. I'm not defending it but I want to walk through it to better understand why this thought is knocking so hard at my consciousness. Waiting for me to acknowledge it.

I feel drawn to and greatly admire those who spend their lives doing for others. Being part of a community. Being a benefit to their community. Like Mia and Garret, like Mason and Emmy. Like everyone I've met who include 'service' as a part of their lives.

I envy those who's lives are based in service. There's a comfort they appear to have, a purpose, that they are aware of. It seems to be fulfilling that call and that awareness is so powerful it shows in their smiles, their energy and their determination. Yes. Do I envy that? To say I am jealous does't seem strong enough. I know to say I am envious means if I can't have it I don't want them to have it. That purpose driven life. So I know I don't mean envy. God knows we need these servants. But I mean something. Maybe I'm jealous and sad. That, combined, feels stronger. I'm sad I don't have that pull. That direction. That understanding of what I am to be doing.

I jumbled more words together and shared it with the world via my blog. I included a picture of the water rushing over the rocks. I am being selfish. I can't defend it. Maybe I shouldn't have to. Except to my own questions about it. But acknowledging it tells me that there is something I need to be doing. I've never known what it is. But at least knowing this much is a start.

As I lay in bed drifting off I can't help but wonder how I get to this age and still have existential thoughts.

I woke to a beautiful morning. I made more tea and went to stand by the river to drink it. That sound, such a tempo. After finishing the tea I walked back and put the cup on the bench. I walked the rutted road that had brought me here. I walked opposite of the direction I came from and past where I had walked to yesterday. I just kept walking. There were other camp spots but only one other that was occupied. About a mile or so from me a small tent was set up with a motorcycle parked nearby. There was no sign of anyone as I walked on by. I came across one camp site that sloped down to the river. I walked down the earthen ramp to the edge of the river. Taking my shoes and socks off I stepped in and walked around the edge. The cold water washed over my feet cooling my entire body. I just stood there. Watching where the water was going. I don't know how long I stood there but my feet hurting from the cold told me to step out. I did and stood on a rock to let my feet dry. When they were dry enough I put my shoes on and walked back, passing the tent and the motorcycle and returned home.

I made an egg and cheese sandwich and sat down at my computer. I was surprised at the number of comments on my post. Well over a hundred. Many of them sharing and acknowledging their own struggles with purpose. I was surprised to come across my first, real, negative comment. Negative because I interpreted the comment as angry, or just not nice. It said "seems like you have a lot to be grateful about and nothing to be complaining about, get over yourself."

I kind of chuckled. I kind of agreed. I kind of thought *what is he so angry about.* I say he because he used 'Tom' as the poster's name. Then I got a little defensive. I don't remember complaining.

I always respond to comments and it took me quite some time to get to Tom's comment. I responded kindly but truthfully. "Thank you Tom. I certainly agree I have nothing to complain about. I don't think what I said was said as a complaint but as an observation. And a willingness to look at my life to see what it's about and what I think it should be about. I am grateful for all that I have and all that I have done. I'm grateful for the ability and willingness on my part to make those things happen. I am not sure what you mean by 'get over' myself but am willing to hear you out. Thanks for reading and commenting." Let's see if Tom has any suggestions for me to get over myself, or a definition of what he meant.

As I finished up with comments and doing a little reading of my own I saw through my window a white haired, white bearded man walking the road. Heading in the direction of the motorcycle tent. He carried a small red plastic gas can.

Initially I thought to let him pass quietly. Something spurred me on to step out and speak to him.

"Hey". He stopped, a little startled.

"Hi. Sorry. Lost in my thoughts. Didn't even see your van." He smiled softly.

"No worries. I just saw you walking. Everything okay?"

"Yes, thank you". He turned as if to continue walking.

"Would you like a hot tea, or coffee. Or pop?"

He hesitated for only a moment. Smiled softly again "that would be very nice. Hot tea if you don't mind."

My turn to smile. "Not at all." He walked over and set his red can at the front of the van. "Are you the tent camper with the motorcycle?" I busied myself getting out my extra chair and placing it with the table between us. I stepped inside and put the kettle on and set out 2 mugs.

"Yes. I've been riding around these last few months. Seeing some beautiful sights". I stuck my head out, he was standing by the chairs. "Please, sit. Is Irish Breakfast Tea good?"

"It's very good!" He lowered himself into the chair. I put some Oreos, cheese and crackers on a plate and brought it out to him. He placed it on the table. "I'll wait for you". He was a little grizzly looking. Hair just a little long. Beard a little too long to manage well but not yet long enough to 'flow'. His t-shirt had the sleeves cut off, his shorts were baggy. His shoes were a nice pair of hiking shoes. He was clean, just grizzly. The best word I can think of.

I got the feeling…something about him felt humble.

I stepped back in the van and poured the not quite fully boiled water into the mugs. Stuck my head out again and said "I'm Bronaugh".

"That's a great Irish name. I'm David." I finished up the tea and brought out our mugs, spoons, sugar and plate to put our tea bags on. Once everything was set on the table I sat across from him. He picked up the mug closest to him and held it out to me. We clicked our mugs and at the same time said "Slainte".

Both of us lifted our eyebrows. He tipped his head in a slight nod. "Have you been to Ireland Bronagh?"

"I have. I stayed for months on an island off the west coast."

"County Galway? County Kerry? Clare? Mayo?" I smiled at his knowledge.

"County Kerry". I was intrigued he asked.

"The Great Blasket?"

Stunned. How did he know? "The one and only."

"Beautiful place."

"You've been?"

Smiling. "I have been and am better for it."

I sat back. Eager to know more but suddenly relaxed with an ease that felt oddly familiar. "It's not often I come across someone who knows of the Great Blasket".

"So, what drew you to her? Peig? To`mas? Or was it Maurice? Or was it Robin Flowers?" As he named the great writers that first told me of this place it occurred to me that though this place was very personal to me it had the ability to draw in others. This made me both sad, because I didn't want to share it and elated because it spoke of the community it depended on. The story of my life. Contradictions.

"It was all of them. In one form or another. I admired their humor. Their toughness. The spirit of community, both good and bad." David nodded along with me. "Tell me about you and the island."

"I went after getting out of prison." He looked at me over his mug. I tried not to react but know my eyebrows betrayed me. He lowered his mug and laughed. "I'm sorry. I shouldn't do that. I wasn't in prison. Though I always told my friends after my divorce it was like getting out of prison."

"So marriage was like a prison?"

"No. It wasn't just the marriage. It was trying to live a life that didn't…" he paused. "I don't know that I can explain it over a cup of tea."

We were both silent for a minute. "We sure did get *there* at warp speed." He grinned and sipped. "We did indeed."

"But, you did go there?"

"I did. I took some time off and spent a few weeks traveling Ireland and Scotland. I spent a couple of nights there in a tent. Best two nights in a tent, of my life". I remembered the tent campers. And sleeping bag only campers. On such a windy and possibly wild weather island, they were definitely taking chances.

"How did you know it was the books that drew me in?"

"Just a guess. Anyone familiar with the island is usually familiar with at least one of the writers. Or they've descended from there."

Over the next hour and another cup of tea we talked about Ireland and our travels here. We seemed to mutually agree not to head back into personal territory. He did indicate he was partially retired. His hope was to spend what he called quality time in each state. He didn't want to just drive through. I told him I was heading down the coast. He gave me some suggestions.

We talked about goals of our travels. Slightly embarrassed I told him I wrote about mine. "Do you share it?" I told him I do and where to find 'me'. He pulled out a large cell phone and with my directions he found my blog. He book marked it. "I'll read it later."

David stood up, picked up his mug and the empty plate, stepped to yellow door and laid them inside on the floor without entering. He knocked on the wooden side of my 'home'. "This is beautiful". He walked back to me and past me. "I need to be going. I thank you for a wonderful visit. I wasn't expecting my morning to be so enjoyable."

"I feel the same". I stood up and we shook hands. We both said "safe travels" and I watched until he walked out of sight.

I sat back down to write about my visit with Motorcycle Tent David. It was such a relaxing and non-pressure filled interaction. A brief encounter with someone, sharing some talk and some tea. So casual and so valuable.

I took my time making a huge salad. I put some chicken breasts on to grill and bagged portions of the salad in sandwich bags for easy grab meals. When the chicken was done I cut one up and tossed into the salad I had left in the bowl. I enjoyed every bite of it as I sat above the river again. I contemplated packing up and leaving but I would be hustling without a plan to find a place to sleep tonight. Back in the van I cut up the rest of the chicken and added it to the bagged salads. With that done I sat with my maps, my tips from Motorcycle Tent David and looked into driving tomorrow and getting to the coast.

I checked my blog comments after my post about Motorcycle Tent David was up for a few hours. I wasn't really surprised to see that others had commented on 'Tom's" comment. Tom had yet to reply to me. I wouldn't be surprised if he didn't.

Bed time came early. As did sunrise. With a cup of tea in hand I went outside and packed up the bench, chairs and table. I opened all of the doors and windows and swept out and wiped out the van. Housekeeping, even in a van, can be tedious.

I walked to the front of the van to open the cab doors and wipe off the dash. There was a piece of paper on the windshield. Instinctively I knew it had to be from David. But I never heard him approach the van.

"Bronagh-

Thank you for the tea and snacks yesterday. More, for the conversation. I read much of your blog last night. I just wanted to add 'my comment' to your blog about purpose and service. Though I understand and can relate to feeling 'selfish'. I want to remind you, or prompt you, to consider a larger definition of service. Personally, I feel service to others comes in many forms. I try to keep a focus on respect and kindness in every day actions to and with others as a form of service. Being kind, interacting with (old guys with scraggly beards!) others and participating in life with others *is* service. Maybe not defined as such, but it doesn't make it less so. I also consider being a good steward to our earth as service. Don't destroy as you go. Clean up after yourselves, and others who don't, are also forms of service. While you try to figure out the 'more' you can and want to do, don't minimize what is is you are doing.

It was a pleasure to meet you. May you be safe in your travels and successful in your seeking.

M.T.Dave"

Well. Well.

Thank you Motorcycle Tent David.

Thank you.

I placed the letter, for safe keeping, in my notebook. Once packed and driving I found myself smiling. Inside and out. It never gets old. The gratitude of being encouraged by others. And having others help you define what it is you are doing and who you are. And that it matters.

VIII.

I drove until I reached the 101, and from there I pulled onto an access road. I drove until I could park, get out, and stand above the Pacific Ocean. Growing up in the middle of America the ocean was not so easily accessible or a part of my life. Then I met the ocean. And I was hooked. Standing here I am, newly and again, made aware of its pull on the human senses.

The sight of it's massive-more-than-we-can-see existence.

The smell of salted air, fish and plant life.

The feel of the ocean based wind, the sand and the rocks.

The sound of water's roll, roar and waves.

The taste of salt, but more, the taste of fresh.

Just to be there, without any actual interaction yet, was satisfying. Observing with all senses could be all overwhelming or calming. Energizing or restful. Depending on the physical, mental and emotional need and wants of the human experiencing it.

I sat so long with the ocean I didn't realize how late it was getting. I started paying attention to those around me. I saw some carrying backpacks disappearing into trees. I followed them. To the beach. Campsites were scattered around. I went back to the van and opened the windows. Surely the vehicles around me belonged to some of these campers. I was staying put. I ate one of the bags of salad in the van then returned to the ocean watching, taking with me my computer and my chair. I was living this moment for the sunset. Until then I emailed friends and studied a little about the 101.

Without being fully aware I had stopped searching or using the computer as it sat blankly on my lap and gradually became aware of people who had sat near me. A young man and a young woman. They were also sitting in chairs. Were they there when I walked back and set up my chair? Or did they arrive after? I closed my computer and stuck it by my side in the chair. I stared straight ahead. Try as I might now that I was aware of them I couldn't help but tune into them.

They spoke casually, they were obviously very familiar with one another. They spoke in normal tones. Not hushed like they didn't want me to hear. I felt guilty but I don't know why. Our proximity to one another almost encouraged us to be in conversation. They seemed to be enjoying their time together. I settled into my chair. Relaxing. Their voices just fit. They were both teenagers. Just graduated. Cousins. They were talking about future plans. The girl was going into an apprentice program to be an electrician. The boy was heading to college. They asked each other if they were scared. They both told the other they were. At least a little bit.

Quite by instinct their voices softened as the sun drew closer to the edge of the world, the water. The colors were mesmerizing. Their voices went silent. As the tip of the sun just touched the horizon, as if it were dipping into the ocean, the two of them emitted soft-simultaneous 'sizzle' sounds. It made me smile.

After awhile they agreed they should get home. They had told grandma they would play cards with her. They were packing up their chairs. I turned to look at them for the first time and softly wished them a good night. They smiled in return and wished me the same.

Nothing more was said between us. I couldn't have asked for better sunset watching company.

I closed up the van but for a crack in one window. The smell was intoxicating. I fell asleep hearing and smelling the ocean. I woke early, before the sun, to remnants of a dream I couldn't quite recall. I made coffee and went out to the dark. I carried my coffee all the way down to the beach. I could see tents but no peoples. I sat with the ocean on a damp rock. As I adjusted to melting into the setting I quietly but pointedly heard 'Go Home.' Ah. From my dream, it was coming back in my thoughts. I stared at the waves and lifted my face to the wind. 'Go home' said my dream. The realization or remembering of my dream was surprising. And strong. Once 'go home' entered my consciousness I couldn't shake it. Details started to become clear. "I" stood in the middle of a street. It was dark and foggy yet I could see clearly. The street was old and lined with beautiful old homes. Some looked like cottages. Some looked like cabins. Some looked like Brownstones you would see in old New York City. At the end of the street, very far away, was a mountain and an ocean. I stood in my dream, and now in the remembering of it, staring. Go home, said the dream. I don't know who's voice it was or where it came from. All I did was stand there. And hear it.

Now, awake, I sat on the wet rock. The ocean, real, but not more so than in the dream. I sat long after my coffee was gone. Then I went home. To the van. And left.

The nice thing about this drive are the towns that someone conveniently put in helpful places for wifi and/or bathroom use. I could tell already this would be a difficult drive. I would rather be looking at the ocean, the views, the towns,   then be the driver.

I hoped for, and found, a small cafe close to the ocean. Walking in, there was a chalkboard sign that had a skilled drawing of a cliff over the ocean and 'local produce only' written under the cliff. It made me think of Mia and Garrett. The cafe was empty so I took a seat by the window. A waiter came from the back and stood over me, handing me a menu and waited for me to order. He didn't say anything. It was a little disconcerting. After ordering a pita stuffed with fresh vegetables and an iced tea I sat quietly looking out the window. Even up here it was salt-spotted by wind carried ocean spray.

My check was brought to me the same time as my meal with a cursory 'no hurry' said as the waiter walked away. Which made me pay more attention to him. Or want to. He disappeared into what must have been the kitchen. The pita was very nice. Refreshing. When I finished I went to the counter to pay. No one was around. I cleared my throat hoping someone would hear me. There was a small pass through window from the kitchen to the front.

I coughed. I finally made out the young man, standing by the back door of the kitchen. He turned and looked at me. He was crying. He just dropped his head. Not sure of what to do, I left money to cover the bill and a tip on the counter. I stuck it under the edge of the computerized cash register.

I walked out to my van but saw a stone walkway that led to stone steps that led to the ocean. I took the steps down until they deposited me on the rocky sand. I took it all in. There were logs and rocks that were well placed for sitting but I'd been sitting. I took a very long walk down the beach. Enjoying the lapping, the coming and going of the ocean. No one else was around.

I made my way back to the steps after more than an hour of walking. The waiter was standing on the beach. On the other side of the stairs in the opposite direction that I had taken. He was just watching the ocean. Hands in his pockets. Head up. Part of me wanted to speak but I wasn't sure I should. I started up the steps when I heard "HEY!" From his direction. I turned and he was heading towards me. I stopped and turned to come back down. He met me. His eyes were direct. His curly hair almost in his eyes. "I'm glad I saw you. I saw your van and thought, hoped, you would be down here."

"Hi."

"Hi. I just wanted to apologize to you. I wasn't very nice in there" tossing his chin up to indicate the cafe.

"No worries." I gave him an understanding smile. I had to consider we all have moments where we haven't been very nice, or wanting to be around others.

"No. Some worries" he smiled. "I mean, I just wanted to say I was sorry. I'm not normally so awful."

"Awful may be an over statement. Maybe...sour?" Again, a smile from him. Though his eyes weren't really involved with the smile.

"Anyway. I hope your pita was good. And..um..thanks". He turned to leave towards the beach. Against my nature I reached out and lightly touched his shoulder. The sad face that turned back to look at me was heart wrenching.

"Uhm…" not sure what was happening. "You look like you could use someone with good ears."

He smiled, still again not a happy smile. He started to decline then said "do you like chocolate shakes?"

"Yes."

"Okay. Come on." He took the steps to pass me. I thought we were returning to the cafe but he walked past it and into a little ice cream shop just up and behind the cafe. He pointed to an outside patio for me to go sit on. Within minutes he returned with two large shakes. Complete with whipped topping and maraschino cherries. He handed me a paper wrapped cardboard straw. The shake was amazing, and thick. I wasn't sure if the straw's life expectancy would see it to the end of the shake.

The young man was paying a lot of attention to his shake. He was barely past being a boy.

"My name is Bronagh".

"Bronagh?"

"Bro-nah".

He repeated it. "Nice. Unusual."

"And you…"

"I'm Robin. My middle name is Williams. Not William. My mom loved the guy."

"A lot of us did. Still do. Can I pay you for the shake?"
"No, my treat. I kind of feel like I owe you."

"You don't owe me anything. I could see you weren't having a good day."

"No. I wasn't. But still no excuse to take it out on you."

"Well, let's put that away. This…" I picked the shake up "more then makes up for it."

"Thanks." He seemed to visibly relax a little.

"It was awfully nice of you to come looking for me. That says a lot about you". He didn't respond. I watched, horrified almost, as a tear rolled down his face. His shoulders shook, softly, he was trying to hold his pain in. Softly so not to intrude but to let him know it was okay I asked "how can I help?" I dropped my hands in my lap and acknowledged his pain.

He raised his hand to his face. "My dad died". He dropped his hands in his lap and dropped his chin to his chest. And sobbed. I pulled his shake away from him and pushed mine to the side. He laid his head on his arms on the table. I sat. Silent. My own tears started falling as I watched this young man let go. I don't know how long we sat there. I grabbed napkins from the dispenser on the table and stuck them in his hand. He pulled back with his head at table level to wipe his eyes and blow his nose. More minutes passed.

Finally, he looked up with a crooked smile and said "wasn't that embarrassing." A statement not a question.

"Not for me." That elicited a small chuckle from him. Though it was intended to let him know his emotions weren't embarrassing.

I told him I would listen, if that is what he needed. He did. He had come to the west coast over a year ago. He wanted to be 'somewhere else' then home. Home wasn't bad. But it had changed. His mother had died years ago. He was an only child. When he was almost 15 his father had remarried. The new wife, she was always kind to him. But it had always been dad and him. Or dad and her. It never, to him, felt like 'us' with all three of them. He came west just for the experience. He didn't have anything to tie him down. His dad, and wife, didn't want him to go. They tried but couldn't understand how he felt. He knows it was him and his perception, or blocking, of feeling misplaced or replaced.

His stepmom was holding off on the service until next week when Robin could get there. He had talked with his dad almost every day since leaving. His death was unexpected, his father was only 53 years old. Robin spoke kindly of his stepmom. But there was something missing. He acknowledged it but he didn't know what it was.

All I could do was listen. So I did. Paying attention to his tone, his eyes, the gradual release of tension. He stopped talking and sat back. Almost slumped. Not exactly a smile appeared but a kind of smile, sat comfortably on his face. "Thank you."

"You're welcome Robin."

I asked what he needed. He said 'nothing'. Just to go home, he had quietly added.

Just as suddenly as I had become a part of this young man's life, it ended. We said goodbye in the parking lot. His sorrow still heavy but having talked about it, maybe he had a reprieve. Or a direction or a way, to take his grief and do what he needed to do in the now. At least for a brief moment.

I felt gratitude at being some place, when I was needed, and could help. I thought about what M.T. David had said about kindness. The importance of my own feeling wasn't lost on me. I drove for some time. Oblivious to the views I was passing.

IX.

I don't know how long I drove but I needed a break and pulled off the road when I saw a sign that indicated beach camping. I checked my app to see if free camping was really available. To my frugal delight it was. I rolled slowly through the parking lot and found an on-sand spot. I wasn't close to the water but close enough to watch it, hear it, walk to it.

There was no one around. Not one single soul. I had the world to myself. I made my way to the ocean and let it fill every part of me. I remained standing in the ocean wind. Alone. Content to be alone. But I knew the longer I stand here alone-the harder it would be to challenge life to be better. Fuller. Different, again.

The ocean was its normal fierce self. Noisy in this silent place. The kind of noise I liked. In the silence I liked. Selfish thoughts started to crowd in. Ah! I need to redefine selfish, to humanly respond to things that give me peace shouldn't be selfish. But still, these thoughts of solitude and discovery do not have to be the only means of fulfillment and joy. I can live like this and be happy. I can live other ways and be happy. Different 'happys'. One way of living, more safe, than the other. Maybe.

I turned and went back to the van. I closed the doors to cook without the wind's intrusive behaviors and to make phone calls without having to talk over the wind. Many phone calls. Surprising myself, and those who I called.

Hannah-come back to Ireland.
Brother-come back to be around family.
Ealga-come back to Ireland.
Leo and Pilar-come see us.
Mia and Garret-do what you need to do.

By the time I had finished talking with everyone I had cooked, eaten and cleaned up. The wind was strong enough to gently nudge the van. I was sitting in my chair with my feet on the bed. When I finally went back outside I had to wear a jacket. I pulled a chair out of the back of the van. I had a text conversation with Maggie. She seemed to prefer text.

My conversation with Robin shook something loose in me. I don't even know for certain what it was. But I felt a need to connect. Most likely the loss he was going through jolted me a little. I thought about my 'people'. It was not lost on me that the people I was most connected with were relatively new to my life. Some relationships only 5-6 years 'old' to me. Other than my brother, sister and their kids I didn't have a long history of staying connected to others. I looked out to the sun hanging low. Clouds were high and far out from the beach. The sun was sandwiched between the clouds and the line of the horizon. Surely a metaphor for something. I sat with my phone stuck in the sand. No talking or texting. Just me and the world. I sat long after the sun set.

When I later posted a picture of my ocean view I wrote briefly about Robin. Not about him exactly. Not his name. Not his story. Or even my encounter with him. I wrote about what I was feeling. Because I suddenly realized I had discovered a lot of what I had hoped to. Not answers to life's perpetual great questions asked ad nauseam over the millenniums. Truthfully I didn't understand enough to even formulate any questions of my own, great or mediocre. But, people. I found them or they found me. We connected for minutes, or hours. Sometimes remaining connected. Sometimes not. When I look back at the things I wrote about, it was either an interaction with someone that made an impression on my thoughts and feelings. Or it was about place. A place that impacted me-through vision.

'Go home.' Again. That thought. I sat on that beach. Freezing. But I didn't want to get up. I wanted to remain by this ocean. But I also don't. Damn my complexities.

I zipped my jacket fully, pulling the neck of it over my chin and mouth, and pulled my arms inside my jacket. I breathed into my jacket and felt some warmth. I stared at the sky. The stars. The intensity of its vastness was both ordinary, because how common an event to look up at the stars, and extraordinary, because-the universe! I stared until I could see the different colors. The variety of stars shapes and brightness.

Eventually I went to the van. Got ready for bed and sat down to review my thoughts, my options. So many choices to be explored or yet discovered. I was pleased with what I had saved and not yet spent. I could continue as I was for quite some time. A year. Possibly longer. Travel. Experience. See. Part of me wanted to do this forever. It wasn't going to last forever though. I wasn't making any real money because I wasn't committed to even the small income sources I had set up when I was with Mia and Garrett.

I took inventory. I took stock. I did whatever it is that people do when they review their lives in full, then move on.

I pulled up my files and opened my maps. I wasn't going to see all I had thought I would. Not right now. And yet I had already gotten more than I thought I would through these travels. As I sat in the van the Pacific Ocean was to my right, technically the Atlantic Ocean was to my left.

By noon the next day I was driving. I went left. With a mental nod to Robert Frost I thought, I have

Miles to go before I have to make decisions. Choices. But I'm going. I suspect the next miles of my life will be different. Better. At least as good as, but likely even better, than the miles in my past. I was going back.

Home.

Thank you for taking the time to read my book.